KING

J.M. DABNEY

EXECUTIONERS BOOK 3

ISBN-13: 978-1-947184-15-2

CONTENTS

Dedication

To my readers, you all make these stories possible.

1 He Was More Than a Flirt and No Name Fuck

Through the applause, Andrew King and his band, Executioners, took one final bow and waved as they walked off stage. He smiled at the loudest one in the crowd. Lincoln Church, his ex-brother-in-law. The man rarely missed one of their shows, but they only really played at Brawlers, a gay bar, on the outskirts of their hometown. The band was more a hobby than anything, none of them had dreams of fame. They were asked plenty when they'd get themselves a contract and live a life as rock stars—that wasn't for them, and two of the reasons waited for his bandmates. He watched his friends as they hurried to their partners.

Ghost was married to Harper, and they had a baby on the way by surrogate. He watched as Ghost scooped the petite Harper into his arms and she seemed to just melt into the man. They exuded enough happiness to fill the whole room.

Joker was married, and it was a full-time job keeping the man out of jail, he felt sorry for Dem, Joker's husband. Dem stayed on his stool and opened his arms. Joker hated being touched but seemed to relax as he walked into his husband's arms. It was nice to see. A lot had changed since Dem came into Joker's life and he couldn't believe how much. Joker even smiled on occasion, well, when the man wasn't scowling and trying to get himself thrown in jail. Sheriff Camden Pelter had a full-time job on his hands just keeping Joker under control. Throw in the rest of the Crews, and he was surprised Camden hadn't run as far and fast from Powers as he could.

Sin and Saint, the youngest of his band, were still single, but they had their eyes on a man who was on the run every time they were around. He didn't doubt the twins would get him eventually. Camden didn't have much choice. The twins were obsessed, and everyone found it amusing except the Sheriff.

But fuck, he was jealous of what his friends found. Everyone thought he was just a flirt and a fuck, but he wasn't. He was just terrified of ruining his friendship with Linc. He loved the man. The whole ex-brother-in-law thing ruined his chance. His ex-wife knew he was gay before he did.

He'd loved his wife, but not in the way she'd deserved. They'd done what was expected when they'd dated for several years, and Melanie ended up pregnant. She was currently off at college while he took care of their son, Mal. She came home on breaks and for the Summer, the occasional weekend. She was actually home this weekend, so she was spending quality time with Mal. Being away from their son killed her, but for him, he wanted her to have every opportunity, and that meant college. For as long as he'd known her, she wanted to be a nurse, and he needed her to take the chance.

They had an odd little family, yet it worked for them.

He stepped up to the bar and took the beer the bartender Twitch handed him with a huge smile. He nodded his thanks and smiled wider as a strong arm circled his waist.

"Amazing as always, King."

Linc gave him a tight squeeze and took his own refill from Twitch.

"Thanks."

Linc let him go, and he almost moved closer to silently ask Linc to put his arm around him again. Linc was the perfect guy. He was sweet, caring, intelligent, handsome, and King loved the man's softness. Linc was a big guy. Shorter than his own six-three, but Linc was chunky, he had this rounded belly that had a bit of a jiggle to it, his arms and thighs thick. Linc was also hairy as fuck. He'd lost count of the times Linc played the main star in all his jerk-off fantasies.

Linc was a science teacher and high school football coach. He never felt quite good enough even to be Linc's friend. Melanie, Linc, and he co-parented Mal since they'd brought the baby home from the hospital.

He drove trucks during the week, sometimes over the road that kept him away for days at a time, but Mal stayed with Linc. He loved when Linc watched Mal at his house because Linc would sleep in his bed. Linc's scent would still be on his sheets when he came home. It was the best sleep he'd have all week.

As some guy came up to him, he frowned as Linc stepped away. He turned his head to ask Linc where he was going only to see the man smiling as he started a conversation with one of the bouncers, Bull. King turned down the invite to head outside. He and the man had hooked up before, but it was getting old not being able to have the one he wanted. It also caused him guilt to be propositioned with Linc so close. They wouldn't ever be more than friends, and that killed a piece of his heart every time he was reminded of it.

Linc always stepped away to allow him space to find someone—to hook up—but that wasn't what he wanted. He had let people think what they wanted, although, it was getting harder to pretend and deny the truth. Melanie knew him better than anyone, and she protected all his secrets no matter how much she hated it.

His phone vibrated in his back pocket, he pulled it out to find Melanie's picture on the screen, and he rushed for the front door. He stepped out into the cool night air and took a long deep breath. The breeze felt good on his overheated skin.

"Hey," he answered.

"Shit, I hate calling you."

"Melanie, don't even start, what's going on?"

He and Melanie had been best friends long before they were a couple or co-parents. Most would probably think their relationship weird, but to them, it was natural to go from husband and wife right back to best friends.

"This is so stupid, but Mal's in bed and I really want ice cream."

He chuckled. "What kind and what else do you need?"

"Just the usual, oh, and you know."

He chuckled, he knew the woman better than he knew himself most days. He sensed her moods even when they were hundreds of miles apart.

"How can you still be embarrassed, we were together for eight years and friends since we were ten."

"Come on, don't make a big deal out of it, I want my fucking ice cream."

"I'll get everything packed up and be home in an hour or so." He walked away from the door as it opened and the overpowering bass of the music inside made it hard to hear.

"Perfect, I have homework to do, and a presentation to prepare for. It's going to be a long night."

"You got this, Melanie."

"I know, see you soon, love you."

"Love you too. We'll take a movie break when I get home." They didn't spend enough time together. He lived under a constant shadow of guilt for the time he didn't have for Mal, Melanie, and Linc. He worked as a trucker to afford to take care of them, so they wouldn't have to work harder than they needed to, but lately the cons were outweighing the pros. He'd been doing it for years, and at thirty, he didn't want to have to find a new job—especially when finding a new one wouldn't be as well-paying as the one he already had.

"Sounds perfect."

"Is Melanie okay?"

He disconnected the call and turned to find Linc behind him. The man looked gorgeous in faded jeans and a v-neck t-shirt that exposed the thick hair that he knew covered the man's chest and stomach. It matched Linc's dark blond hair.

"She wants ice cream."

"Do you want me to take care of it so you can finish up here?"

The man was selfless, Linc was always the first one to offer to help. He did it without even thinking of getting paid back. He didn't even expect a thank you.

"No, do you want to help me pack up? It was a rough week. I'd just like to go home."

"Sure. Are you okay? Want to talk about it?"

"I'm fine, I just think I need a vacation, and I might do that later this Summer. We can go somewhere."

And by *we* he included Linc and Melanie because to him, it was always the four of them.

"That would be good for you, Melanie and Mal."

He didn't correct him, Linc still tried to give him and Melanie space when she was in town. It was as if he didn't want to intrude on their time with Mal. Linc was always included. He and Melanie had talked about it, Linc was as much a father to Mal as he was.

"Want to come over and watch a movie with Melanie and me, like the old days?"

"That would be great. I'll make breakfast."

"Deal."

They headed back inside and made quick work of breaking everything down with Joker and Ghost helping. Sin and Saint had taken off to stalk the Sheriff who was seated in a back corner having a beer by himself. The man had company he hadn't expected. Finally, they had the van packed up and said their goodbyes.

"Meet you at the house," Linc called as he hopped into his car.

He watched until Linc was inside and the man pulled out of the parking lot, heading in the direction of his cabin. He jumped into the van and drove off toward town. His mind wandered to places it shouldn't. He loved Melanie. She'd been his best friend in high school, and when they'd started dating, it seemed like the thing to do. Melanie was bisexual, she'd told him early on in their friendship, but her family wasn't accepting, and neither was his. He'd felt like such a hypocrite when he hadn't shared he was gay. When they'd had sex, it hadn't been fireworks, but they'd had a great relationship. They never argued. When she'd come to him and asked him if he was gay, she hadn't been angry when she asked, more disappointed that he hadn't confided in her.

They'd divorced but continued to live together. It was natural. They'd grown impossibly closer. Nothing really changed except they didn't share a bed anymore. They'd agreed to never keep secrets from each other, but he didn't know how she'd handle knowing her ex-husband and best friend had been in love with her brother for years.

He'd wanted to tell her and ask for advice, but he didn't want to deal with the weirdness that might come from it.

He turned into the parking lot of the only twenty-four-hour gas station in town. He got out and hit the alarm, he strode across the parking lot to get what Melanie needed, then head home to his family.

2 Lincoln Shouldn't Be There

Linc downed another glass of ice cold water and tried not to stare into the living room. The doorway perfectly framed King who was seated on the couch, Linc's sister's head rested on King's thigh. That's the way he'd left them a few minutes ago. He shouldn't be there, but he couldn't help himself. No matter how many times he'd tried to ignore his love for his former brother-in-law, it wouldn't go away.

He could almost pretend they were an actual family, him, King and Mal. He loved his nephew like his own. During the week when King was on runs, he'd leave work and go pick Mal up from the babysitter. They'd spent the afternoon at the park or playing, they'd have dinner, and then call King to say goodnight. Sometimes he and King would talk after Mal went to bed.

When the calls would end, he'd close his eyes and pretend King was beside him. The worst nights were when he was curled up in King's bed. Surrounded by King's things and his scent, oh, how many times had he resisted the urge to stroke one out. He felt his face heat and poured himself another glass of water.

He smiled as Mal ducked into the kitchen rubbing his sleepy eyes, he was a mini-version of King. He walked forward and picked Mal up, the kid's big boy bed made it easier for Mal to come search them out. He'd nearly had a heart attack the first night he'd watched him after they'd got him the bed and didn't find Mal tucked under the covers.

He'd found him on the couch curled up under King's huge leather jacket asleep. King had laughed his fool head off when he told the man the story.

It had hurt his feelings for a split second. He'd always been a bit on the fat side his whole life and men had made a habit of laughing at him. That wasn't King. He'd felt like an asshole for the small slip. The man was adamant that he was a handsome guy and bitched him out more times than he could remember for putting himself down.

He cradled Mal to his chest and carried him into the living room, King looked up and patted the spot beside him. He started to lay Mal down, but King pulled them both down. Mal stayed on his lap but leaned his head against King's bicep. His heart kicked up a few notches as King laid his arm on his lap and took Mal's left hand. He noticed Melanie tilted her head back to look at them. She seemed so content.

He scooted down enough to put his feet on the coffee table and settle in to finish watching the action movie King and Melanie chose.

King and Melanie held hands, she giggled when King tickled her, and he tried to focus on the movie.

He remembered the first time he'd seen King. He'd moved back to Powers to take over a teaching position at the local high school. The Saturday after he'd settled into his apartment, he'd driven across town to his parent's place.

In the front yard, mowing the grass stood the most beautiful man he had ever seen. He sat in his car and watched. The quickness of his attraction took him by surprise but not nearly as much as the hurt when Melanie came out of the house and wrapped herself around the young man.

"I should go home," he whispered so as not to wake Mal which was stupid with the movie blaring.

King turned, and his long goatee tickled the side of his neck.

"What, why? You always crash here."

"Melanie's home for the weekend, you two should—"

"No, you're staying, no need to go home."

"Come on, Linc, stay, I don't get to see you enough," Melanie pleaded as she stuck out her bottom lip.

"Don't do that, you know I can't say—"

Whatever he was going to say ended when he was subjected to King and Melanie pouting at him. For nearly a decade, they'd struck him weak with those twin pouts. He could understand why they'd stayed best friends so long. They were nearly identical in temperament.

"You want me to put Malcolm to bed," King started to get up.

"No, he's fine."

He tightened his arms around his nephew. His family life hadn't turned out easy after he came out when he left for college. Melanie always stood beside him and made sure he knew he had her support. The Don't Ask Don't Tell rule made family functions uncomfortable. They ignored Melanie's bisexuality. She'd married and given their parents a grandchild. It wasn't like he hadn't dated over the years, and he'd thought for a brief time he'd found the man of his dreams; that hadn't turned out to be the case.

The breakup was amicable. They hadn't been suited. He had wanted different things from life. Marriage, kids, romance, Denny wasn't ready for any of that and hadn't been sure he would've ever gotten to that point.

He had the life he wanted, he had Malcolm, and he was allowed an active role in his nephew's life—almost like a dad. The only dark spot of it all was he didn't have King.

Andrew King was perfect. Caring. The perfect father. King always made him feel included.

His life was Mal, his job, and King, the small family they'd made together.

"You've been quiet, not unusual, but, are you okay?"

He turned toward King and noticed Melanie was asleep, curled up on her side with her face buried against King's stomach. Jealousy of his sister made him feel petty and bitchy.

"Just tired."

King squeezed his knee and shifted closer. King had taken a shower when he got home, and he smelled of a spicy soap scent. A shirtless King was a sight to behold. Bulky, powerful muscles, King didn't have a washboard stomach, but firm and hinted at abs. King had a thick mat of chest hair.

He had wanted the man too damn long. Nights like these were the hardest because they gave him an idea of what belonging to King would be like and it turned painful when he had to walk away.

"Why not go get in my bed? I'll get Melanie settled in her room."

He opened his mouth, then closed it again, clenching his teeth. In bed with King, it was like a dream come true.

No, he couldn't do that, it would be too much temptation and being around King while the man fully clothed was bad enough.

"You can't sleep on the couch."

King was a restless sleeper. A few nights he had come out to check on King and found the man sprawled and cursing where he'd rolled face first onto the floor.

"We can share then. Plenty of room."

"Maybe I can crash with Melanie."

"You forget she's a kicker?"

He chuckled. "There is that. Mal sleeping with us?"

"Of course, he's still not used to sleeping in his own bed. I screwed up when I let him sleep with me since he was a baby."

He held onto Mal as he tried to get up, he started to fall back onto the couch, but the large, strong hand on his ass pushing him back up caused him to tense. His mind went blank, and he searched for anything to say, what had they been talking about? Yes, Mal, the baby was a safe subject.

"He'll develop some independence when he gets older."

King let out a heavy sigh. "I know, you two go to bed and I'll get Melanie up."

"You should just carry her, once she's asleep she's done for."

"That was the plan. I don't see how she does it."

He walked toward King's bedroom, he entered and found the bed already turned down. He laid Mal down and went to King's dresser to find something to sleep in. He had just pulled out pajama bottoms and a t-shirt when he heard King walk in.

He glanced over his shoulder in time to catch King stripping down to red boxer briefs that hugged the curves of his muscular ass. King casually tossed his sweatpants into an overflowing hamper. He mentally made a note to take care of the laundry while King was away working next week.

"I thought you'd be in bed already," King said as he passed behind him and dropped a quick kiss to the side of his neck.

He clenched the fabric in his hands and resisted the urge to moan.

"I was just—" He cleared his throat. "Getting something to wear."

"Go get ready."

He turned to watch King get in bed and gather Mal to his chest. He leaned back against the dresser as he studied King and Mal. He shook his head. King could've had Mal on his own. He never saw much of Melanie in Mal. Where his sister was a blonde and blue-eyed, Mal had wavy black hair and green eyes, exactly like King.

They were so cute together, and he loved them both so much. He knew one day King would find someone, as much of a player as King seemed that wasn't the man he saw. He knew the amazing father and friend that King became, and he was proud of him.

He didn't want King to catch him standing there, so he headed to the bathroom to change. One day he'd have to let King and Mal go, but until then, he'd enjoy the time he had with them. He'd deal with the heartbreak later.

3 Don't Start, Melanie

The sun barely started to illuminate his bedroom when he awoke. His son was spread out, arms and legs splayed in all directions, but he moved his attention from Mal to Linc who was asleep on the opposite side of the bed. So many years he'd wished to wake up like that, Linc beside him. When he'd suggested Linc sleep with him, he hadn't expected the man to say yes. It had taken him forever to fall asleep because he had watched Linc.

His mind wandered back to the day he had met Linc and where his guilt had begun.

"Lincoln," Melanie squealed as she pulled out of his arms and ran across the yard.

He turned to see where she was going. Lincoln was his girlfriend's brother. He let out a loud laugh as she launched herself at a chunky man.

"Hey, short stuff, someone would think you missed me."

He flinched at what that deep, rough voice did to him. Even the deepness couldn't hide the soft shyness of the man's tone. He forced a smile when Melanie spun and wrapped her arm around the man. They approached, and he rubbed his sweaty palms on his denim covered thighs.

"Andrew, this is my brother, Lincoln, Linc, this is my boyfriend, Andrew."

He hesitated as Lincoln extended his arm and offered his hand. He forced his hand not to shake as he took Lincoln's. The man's palm was covered with thick callouses, and his handshake was firm. A vision of having those hands on him formed in his mind, and he broke the contact.

"Nice to meet you, Andrew, Melanie's told me a lot about you over the years."

"You, too. Melanie told me you just moved home."

"Always my intention to do so, but I had to wait for a position to open."

"Come on, Lincoln. Mom and Dad have been waiting for you."

He gave the man a small smile and relaxed as Melanie and her brother disappeared inside. He attempted to take deep even breaths as he tried to calm himself. The man's cologne lingered, and he closed his eyes, savored the scent. Guilt washed over him for his attraction, but what caused him the most pain was he couldn't deny his urges.

"Y'all three looks so cute together."

Melanie's voice and the feel of her rounded chin resting on his bicep brought him back to the present.

"Don't start, Melanie."

"Come on, King, it's not like I didn't know."

When he started to roll from the bed, Melanie stepped back, and he got up to push her out of the room.

"We talked about this."

"And I think I've told you a hundred times, if not more, that I don't care if you're in love with my brother."

He strode quickly to the kitchen to start the coffee. Melanie drank it but she made the worst coffee, always had. Ignoring Melanie was a no-go, the woman didn't know how to mind her own business. So, they'd talked about it, and she didn't seem to have a problem with his feelings for Lincoln; that didn't mean he was altogether comfortable with them, especially since they developed before they'd divorced.

"Quit being a fucking martyr. You were my best friend before you were my husband, but always gay. I'm sure there were other men you found attractive before and after Linc."

"Those were different. They weren't Linc. He's—"

"Special? Then what the fuck is the problem? We've been co-parenting for three years. He's pretty much your partner in every aspect but the sex one. It's the sex isn't it?"

"Do we have to talk about this?"

"Yes, because I'm tired of you beating yourself up for how you feel. When we divorced, we promised no more secrets between us. Our happiness is important to raising an emotionally healthy child. And do you want to end up like Bear?"

"Don't even start in on Bear. My uncle is fine."

"He's after a woman who tried to knife him during a bar fight."

"It wasn't a bar fight. Mary just wasn't prepared when Bear came up behind her."

"Yeah, yeah, I know that, but come on, he's like some teenager with his first crush. You mention her name, and he turns bright red."

He was happy to turn the conversation to his uncle. The man had been a late in life surprise for his grandparents. There was only a ten-year difference in their ages. Bear had a thing for one of King's friend's mothers.

It was kind of cute, to be honest. Mary had been severely abused and tortured by her first and only husband. It wasn't going to be easy for Bear to get her to agree to a date; it was turning out to be damn near impossible.

"We know what happened to her and Joker."

"I understand that, but is she ever going to be able to deal with your hyper-affectionate uncle. The man will hug anybody."

That was true. Bear was too nice to be single. The man would make someone the perfect partner, and he couldn't remember the last time his uncle had a date. In some ways, he thought Bear was starved for attention, he was a huge bear, hence his nickname, of a man. Bear sometimes didn't realize his own strength. The man wouldn't hurt a fly, he was a florist for fuck's sake, but sometimes in his enthusiasm, he'd sometimes forgot people had personal space.

"I heard she actually might have said yes to a date or being his friend. I think he'd be happy with just about anything she offered. He thinks she's adorable."

Melanie snorted, "He would. But don't think I forgot about our conversation. What happens when he finds someone?"

He reached into the cupboard to grab coffee mugs and gripped one a little too tightly at the thought of Linc with someone else—touching someone else or loving them.

He ignored her as she turned to lean back against the counter beside him.

"You should see your face. He's a great guy. How long do you think he's going to remain single? Helping us raise Malcolm? One day he'll want a family of his own."

"He has a family, me and—"

"Maybe he wants to be a dad instead of just an uncle."

He hated to admit she was right, but he couldn't forget all the times Linc talked about having a husband and children. It was all a matter of time, and he didn't know how he'd survive with the man he loved with someone else.

"Maybe after being away this week, I'll get someone to watch Mal, and take Linc out on a date."

"You going to tell him it's a date or just hope he notices? You know Linc is oblivious when it comes to you. For a big, badass man, you're sort of a wimp, never thought I'd see the day that the great and confident Andrew King would be terrified."

"You know how scared I was when I came out. I lost all my family except Bear."

"They were assholes."

He snorted as she hoisted herself onto the counter and leaned to the side to peer up at him.

"At least your family doesn't pretend that you never came out at all. They keep asking Linc when he's going to meet a nice woman and have some kids."

In some ways he had it better, yes, his parents and siblings didn't talk to him anymore, but at least he didn't have to deal with the disrespect of being asked about a nice girlfriend or wife. Linc always came home from the visits almost in tears. The first few times he'd left Linc alone because he'd assumed that's what the man wanted. When he caught Linc crying the first time, he'd hugged him, then held Linc while he sobbed.

"Go wake your man up while I get breakfast started."

She turned him around, then kicked him in the ass to get him moving.

"Snuggle with your man."

"You know, my ex-wife trying to push me at her brother is just weird."

"I was your best friend before your wife, now do as I say."

He rolled his eyes and strode from the kitchen, and he returned to his bedroom. He walked to Linc's side of the bed and sat down on the edge, his hip pressed against Linc's lower back. The man was everything he'd always wanted. He tensed as Linc turned over and Linc's arm wrapped around his thighs.

Linc's sandy blond hair tempted him, so he raised his hand and ran it through the soft strands that were short but shaggy enough to tangle around his fingers. The man's beard brushed his forearm, and Linc's beard was just rough enough he started wondering what it would feel like against his skin. It wasn't the first time. He'd spent a lot of time fantasizing about fucking Linc and being fucked by him. He'd never bottomed before, never had any urge to except with Linc.

"What time is it?" Linc's voice gruff.

He nearly lost it as Linc's bearded cheek rubbed against his bare thigh. Maybe he should've grabbed pants before waking Linc up.

"Too early for a weekend, but your sister is making breakfast."

"Melanie didn't make the coffee, did she?"

"No, I did that."

"Thank you."

Linc's full lips caressed his leg, and he rolled from bed like nothing happened.

He pulled the covers back over Mal and focused on his son as Linc left the room. Mal was the best thing he'd ever done in life. He constantly worried about fucking up, but that wasn't anything new. He lived in a loop of panic that he wouldn't do right by his family.

Sometimes that's why he kept himself from letting Linc know how he felt about him. He loved the dynamic they'd created over the years. Would his confession ruin it all? He couldn't live with that, but he also couldn't go on like he was. Next weekend, he'd take Linc out like he'd told Melanie and take the leap. Knowing had to be better than this. He eased off the bed and went to the kitchen to join Melanie and Linc.

4 King Was Acting Weird

The last load of laundry was shoved into the washer, Linc measured in detergent and then closed the lid. Malcolm was tucked into bed. Dishes were done and put away. Melanie and King left that morning. King dropped Melanie back off at school and then headed off for a long run to Los Angeles.

He hated when King drove that far. He knew King had been at his job for almost nine years. As far as he knew except for the time it took away from Malcolm, King loved his job. He glanced at the clock and found it was almost ten. King always called by then to say goodnight to Mal and talk to Linc for a while.

He didn't have anything else to do but wait for the clothes to finish. Walking through the house, he made sure everything was locked up and lights were turned off before he headed to King's room.

The bed was already turned down. He should sleep in his sister's room, but curling up in King's bed was his guilty pleasure. The closest he'd ever come to King. He went to King's dresser and pulled out pajama bottoms. He changed and bent to pick up the discarded clothes as his phone started to ring. He strode to where his phone was plugged in on the nightstand on the right side of the bed.

"Hello," he answered without checking the caller ID.

"Hey, sorry, pileup put me behind schedule."

King sounded tired.

"It's fine. I told Mal you were probably driving, and it wasn't safe for you to call."

"Thanks, I hate not being able to call, but—"

"The money is better for the over the road trips."

"Yeah. How was y'all's day?"

"Went to the school to pick up my schedule. Picked up the roster for tryouts and to see who's returning this season. Mal came along with me, then we went to the park and had lunch. Then we came home to catch up on laundry."

"Honey, you don't have to do the laundry."

Something happened to him when King used endearments. He'd never liked partners in the past who tried it, but with King, it felt right. It made him feel special because he'd been around King enough when the man was flirting to know he didn't use them with anyone else.

He smiled and shook his head, "When is it going to get done then?"

"I would've done it when I got home."

"Then you'd have twice as much laundry...that you wouldn't do."

King laughed. "Okay, you've got me there."

He turned and sat down on the edge of the bed, he lay back and stared up at the exposed beams of the ceiling. He loved King's cabin. He still lived in the same apartment he'd rented when he moved back.

"What are you doing? You got awful quiet."

"Nothing, lying on your bed and staring up at the ceiling. I need to find a house."

There was silence, and he pulled the phone away from his ear to check to make sure the call was still connected.

"Why? I thought you liked your apartment."

"I like your house more."

"Move in."

"What?"

"Move in. You spend more time there than at your place."

"I couldn't do that."

"Just think about it. There's the empty guest room."

"I'll think about it."

"Which is Linc-speak for no."

He had to admit he did spend more time there than he did at his place. He even had drawers and more than half of King's closet, not that he wore any of it. Most times he grabbed King's clothes to sleep in. A yes tripped on the tip of his tongue. Yes, he'd love to live there, but could he live with King and remain sane. It wasn't a guarantee. He had wanted King for too long. When it seemed like he couldn't resist telling King what he felt, he escaped back to his apartment with some excuse.

"I had an idea."

"Oh, and what might that be?"

"You and me, dinner this weekend. Ben and Psycho said they'd keep Mal. He can play with Gunner and Rage."

"They have to stop calling Thomas Rage. He has two perfectly good names, Hendrix or Thomas. He won't answer to his real name when it's time to start school this fall."

Psycho worked as a bouncer at Brawlers and was married to Ben who owned a Bakery in town. Ben and Psycho co-parented Rage, Gunner, and Sawyer with Psycho's ex-wife and her current wife. It was a weird little family, but it worked for them. He shouldn't call it weird, he acted as a parent with Mal, along with Melanie and King. They'd done it for what seemed like forever.

"You try telling Psycho that and Rage is a perfect name for the little terror."

"He's not so bad, him and Gunner are like super sweet with Mal."

"They are. So what do you say, is it a date?"

Date, he wished that word meant more than a figure of speech. He wanted a real date.

"Sure."

"Great, so it's a date."

His brows drew together at King's emphasis on the last word. It had just hit him. King was acting weird. It wasn't anything overt, the offer for him to move in, now, a night out for the two of them. Unless it was a gig at Brawlers, all their outings were with Mal.

"Is there something you want to talk to me about?"

"No, no, you take care of Mal most of the time, I thought it would be nice to take you out for dinner and whatever else you want to do."

"Okay."

"I better get going, I'll call in the morning to talk to Mal."

"Goodnight, King."

"You too, baby."

The call ended, but he remained on the bed with his phone still pressed to his ear. King's abrupt goodbye like a solid punch to the gut. They spoke for an hour and sometimes more, yet he didn't get to grow sleepy with King's gruff voice in his ear—King's scent surrounding him.

Excuses formed in his mind, King was sleepy, and it had turned into a long day for the man.

He lifted his phone and stroked his fingertip across the screen, finding his sister's number. He tapped the green call button. He bit his bottom lip as he waited for her to answer.

"Hey, Linc."

"Hey, sis."

"Is everything okay?"

"I can't just call you because I want—"

"Shut the fuck up, you know you can, but you know you never do. Unless you want to share a Mal milestone with me."

"I'm sorry, I just…I feel off tonight."

"Issue with King?"

"Why would it be an issue with him?"

"You do know that I've always known you had a thing for King, right?"

Panic tightened his chest as he searched his mind for stupid clues he might've given away over the years. Times he'd paid too much attention to the other man. He braced himself for anger and censure for feelings he'd fought since he'd met the man.

"What the hell are you talking about?"

"Don't try to play innocent with me, big brother."

"How?"

He couldn't deny it, he and Melanie hadn't lied to each other before. So, he'd lied to her by omission for years, and she somehow knew it. He wanted to know how and if King suspected, he'd be mortified. Maybe that's why King wanted to take him out, wanted to warn him that his feelings weren't—

"Are you listening to me, Lincoln?"

"What? Sorry, what were you saying?" He couldn't lose anyone else, his parents gave up on him, but Melanie and Mal, along with King were all he had left in the world. Losing them would kill him, and he was sure he'd never recover from it.

"You don't hide it all that well."

"Fuck—"

"Oh, we're cussing now?"

"Shut up, does he know?"

"Clueless, so you're safe, so don't start getting all embarrassed and shit."

"Why aren't you mad?"

She knew, shouldn't she be pissed that he didn't just have a thing for King, he was in love with the man. It was her ex-husband, and besides being his best friend, Melanie was his sister. This couldn't get any more awkward.

"King was and is my best friend, one night, a few too many drinks, and things went a bit far. We were sixteen, had sex, and we just thought, I don't know what we thought. We loved each other, but not in the way we should've. And when I found out I was pregnant, we'd already fallen into a comfortable space. We did the right thing. When we stood there and said I do to each other, I think…"

"What?"

"We knew it wasn't right. After that, there was no more sex, and we somehow went back to best friends. It wasn't awkward. We stuck it out for a year as we quietly planned getting divorced. We decided I should go to school like I wanted. I knew he was gay. I feel like a bitch keeping him around and not letting him find the man of his dreams, but it is what it is."

"Are you sure he doesn't know?"

Melanie laughed so hard she snorted. "I'm positive he doesn't know. Are you ready to do something about it?"

"No," he shouted.

"Why not? My ex-husband is hot as fuck. And hung, oh, how hung."

"You're just making this weird now."

"It's not a monster or anything, but you sure know—"

"Melanie, what about weird do you not understand?"

"You're too easy, big brother. Why the sudden call?"

"He called tonight, but he was just off. We normally talk for an hour or so in the evenings. I tell him about Mal's day and mine...talk about his. Then he said he wanted to take me out this weekend. Maybe he knows, and he wants—"

"I can guarantee that I would know if he knew. King tells me everything."

He pushed a relieved sigh through his compressed lips. He didn't handle embarrassment well, and he was too attached to Mal and King. Being with them was like living his dream, except the point of not being able to call King his.

"Linc, don't panic. It's probably a thank you dinner for all that you do. We probably don't tell you enough how much we appreciate you being there for us and especially for Mal. It's hard being away from Mal, for both of us.

King with his job and me with school, you give our, and I mean ours, yours, mine and King's son, the normal life he deserves. We love you for that, and we know how much time it takes from finding someone—"

Tears filled his eyes at Melanie calling Mal theirs. It was everything he'd always wanted. He loved Mal like his own and wouldn't know what to do without him.

"I'm happy. I don't feel like I'm missing out. I love that I can have Mal to myself. The highlight of my day is being able to pick him up from daycare and take him to the park or whatever. Making him dinner, reading him his bedtime story. Then I get to talk to King and tell him—"

"Linc, just don't play martyr with this. You deserve to be happy and find someone. If you want King, go for it. Don't hesitate because of mine and King's past."

"Okay, I better let you go, you have classes and probably homework to do."

"Homework is done, but I have a shift at the restaurant in the morning before my first class. I love you, big brother. Do what's right and get your man."

The conversation ended quickly leaving him with more questions than answers. He wanted King, but he couldn't take the chance of losing what he already had. Being King's friend and Mal's parent was more important. He tossed his phone aside and got up to check the clothes and get some sleep.

5 Why Wasn't This Easier?

The volume levels in the truck stop restaurant were enough to give him a headache, but the coffee was good, and the food wasn't drowned in grease so he wouldn't complain too much. He loved his job. He could afford a good life for Mal. It wasn't like he saw exotic places, but he drove through some pretty country. It gave him time to think—sometimes too much.

He let his gaze travel around the crowded room. It could've been any one of a hundred stops he'd made over the years. The faces blended, but occasionally you'd see a familiar one. A big, burly guy sat across the room from him. An old hook up, but he couldn't call the man a friend with benefits. They hadn't made eye contact, but in his gut, he knew the man would approach him or send him a look to signal to him to meet outside. That wasn't what he wanted. Sex turned into the only way he'd allowed himself to be needed. Every experience ended in disappointment and a sharp explosion of self-loathing. He and Linc weren't an item, maybe never would be, yet that didn't change the fact he'd felt as if he cheated on Linc.

All the years that had passed since he accepted he was gay, he'd wasted them on other men out of fear. He couldn't do that anymore. Yet he didn't understand how to move forward.

Why wasn't this easier? He pushed his empty plate to the other side of the table.

He'd thought coming out would've made him happy—instead, he'd felt trapped. A friend of his, Bull, had told him the story of his coming out. It was similar to his. Bull had decided he couldn't hide anymore. His friend's story had helped him accept that not everybody's moment of self-acceptance was the same.

Voicing aloud that he was gay was the right decision, he knew it was. Although, this wasn't how he'd pictured his life four years later.

Every time he'd opened his mouth to tell Linc how he felt about him—nothing came. Fear choked back his confession; he'd lost everyone he'd assumed loved him except Bear. The older man had been his rock. Loved him through the banishment. Bear even cut ties with the family over their disowning him. His mother, Bear's sister, and uncle were always close. Best friends and it had hurt when he'd ruined that.

"Hey, man." The big, burly trucker he'd hoped would ignore him sat down on the other side of the table.

"Hey, Nox."

"You look like you got some shit on your mind."

"It's nothing."

Nox rapped his knuckles on the tabletop. They didn't know each other well, but Nox seemed lighter. Nox's deep scowl a little softer.

"We got a few hours to kill."

"I'm not—"

The man snorted and shook his head. "I ain't talking about fucking. Found a cute little thing who doesn't mind my shitty schedule."

His gaze fell to the man's ring finger to find a thick gold band.

"Congratulations."

"Thanks. So, talk it out."

"I fell in love with my ex-wife's brother."

"Complicated."

"Not so much, really. My ex, Melanie, we've been best friends since we were kids. We're still best friends, and she's been trying to get me to ask Linc out for years."

"Then what the fuck's the problem? Doesn't seem the ex has an issue, so what about the ex-brother-in-law?"

He took a sip of his coffee trying to get his thoughts together, but it was all chaos and mixed emotions in his head. He knew what he felt for Linc, there wasn't any doubt in that department, but would the man see him as lacking.

"Never told him." He woke his phone up and turned it toward Nox. The background of the screen was a recent picture of Linc and Mal. One he'd taken before he'd left on this run.

"You got a cute family there."

"He takes care of Mal while I'm away. Melanie is— why am I telling you this?"

"Why not? Strangers tend to be impartial when it comes to all this shit. I'm sorta returning the favor. Six months ago, I sat in a place similar to this in Mississippi. Some old dude bought me a beer. Said I looked like I had problems I needed to talk out." A wide smile spread across the man's mouth, and Nox scrubbed a hand over his beard.

"Did you?"

"I had plenty of problems. My younger brother's best friend to be exact. Things got a little out of hand one night, and the next morning before he woke up, I ran. Took every run my company wanted to send me on. Stayed away for a month only to come home to find my little man camped out in my house."

King laughed and shook his head. It reminded him of his friend and bandmate Joker and his husband, Dem. Joker ran too, but when he got back, Dem was there waiting to claim his man.

"Seems to have all worked out for you."

"It did. So, what's your issue then? Seems to me you got all the playing house down. He takes care of your—"

"Ours." The urge to correct anyone who used yours when it came to who Mal's parents were turned into an automatic response. "Melanie and me were always clear that Linc was as much a parent as the two of us. He's practically raised Mal. Our kid is amazing because of him. Melanie can pursue her dream of going to college. And me, I can work a job that provides well for us. I can't imagine life without him, and that's what scares the fuck out of me. That he won't be there if he knew."

"What happens if he finds out and he wants the same? It could be a win-win, or least you can find out so you can move on."

"All the advice sounds easy enough, but it really ain't."

"Because you're thinking about all the shit that you shouldn't do. Answer me one fucking question without putting all your bullshit doubts into it. What do you want?"

"Linc."

"Then you know exactly what you need to do. But tonight, man, you gotta play."

He was thankful for the change in subject. He sensed Nox had reached his limit with all the warm and fuzzies or relationships advice.

"The bar out back has got the shittiest open mic night. The diner is busy because everyone escaped."

"Can't be that bad."

"Oh, it's bad. I got no talent whatsoever, but even I know those fuckers are slaughtering everything."

He was thankful for the distraction and the way Nox didn't make shit weird. And the mean ass trucker looked happy. He'd admit he was a bit jealous. He and Nox were similar in attitude and looks, and their past hookups mainly carried out because of boredom.

"So get your fucking guitar and come on."

"Fine, let me take care of my check, and I have to run to my truck."

"Meet you over there. But call your man first, just to say hi."

He shook his head as Nox disappeared. It was weird taking advice from someone he'd fucked, especially one who looked like Nox. Hell, he had Melanie and Nox telling him what he should do, and it was fucked up they knew more about what needed to happen than he did.

He grabbed the check off the table and went to pay. Linc and his last conversation had been a bit awkward; it could be his own insecurities—like talking—but he didn't think so. He took care of the check and walked outside. On the way to his rig, he pulled out his phone and hit Linc's speed dial, then listened to it ring.

"Hey, you're calling early."

"Yeah, I got roped into playing some open mic night thing. Seems it's a nightmare at the bar."

"You know, you never told me why you never tried to go all world-famous musician."

"Because playing is fun and I don't want it to be a job. Besides, being away driving is bad enough, leaving y'all for months at a time would kill me."

"We might miss you a bit."

"Asshole, you're all heart. Where's our kid?"

"Last I heard he was being held hostage by his twin bodyguards. Playdate with the Crew hellions."

He tried not to be disappointed that Mal was away again. Yet he also knew Linc needed a break and some alone time. Linc was full-time dad most of the time, and in some ways, he was jealous of the time Linc spent with Mal. He just didn't know if he could find another job that would pay as well as the one he had.

"Our kid has a better social life than I do."

"That he does. Oh, Melanie called, she had a date."

When he reached his truck, he spun and leaned back against it. "Do tell."

"Seems it's a regular at the restaurant, always sits in her section and Melanie sounded excited about the date."

"Did you call Little to do a background check?"

"No, and we're not going to. She still hasn't forgiven you for that one."

"It was one damn time. And the guy looked shady as fuck."

The guy had seemed nice enough, but he hadn't paid attention to Mal. The bastard had appeared annoyed when Melanie held Mal and didn't give the guy her full attention. Some people didn't do well with kids. He'd gotten Little to do a quick check. One time and they still didn't let him forget.

"Um, have we forgotten what our friends look like?"

"Not the point, Linc, not the point."

"It was definitely the point. She brought him to meet us, and what happened, you sicced Psycho and Livingston on him. The man couldn't run away fast enough."

He chuckled as he remembered the look on the guy's face when he'd gotten out of the car to a yard full of bikers.

"Just proved he wasn't right for her."

"Well, you'll have to sic Lily or Peaches, maybe one of the others on this one."

"We finally get a girlfriend? Good, she has terrible taste in men."

"She married you."

"Yeah, her gay best friend."

"I'm not going to win this one."

"No, you're not."

"Why I love you, I don't have a clue."

King had heard it many times over the years, I love you, man, or some variation, but each time it struck him momentarily speechless.

"Because I'm cute?"

"Maybe, but not that cute. You going to be home Friday or Saturday?"

"Should be in late Friday. We still on for dinner Saturday?"

"Of course. A grown-up dinner, and I'll need to recover from vegan overload. Playdate is at Psycho's place."

"Sorry."

He wasn't really. He was happy that he didn't have to suffer through some tofu-based hell. He still had nightmares about the black bean veggie burger he'd had to choke down the last time.

"No, you're not. Go play and don't make me have to come bail you out."

"I've never had you come bail me out, and the one time you did, that was only because Dem wasn't around to keep Joker out of trouble."

"Whatever, just do as I say."

"Yes, dear."

They said their goodbyes, and he retrieved his guitar case, then made his way toward the little cement building in back. Playing soothed him when he needed to think or everything became too much for him. He'd made his decision, now, all he needed was to have the balls to go through with it. On the one hand, he'd get everything he'd always wanted. But on the other, he could lose it all. Two more days and he'd know if he stood a chance with the man of his dreams.

6 A Crews' Kids' Playdate

"Peace, what have you done?"

Priest yelled at his son, but the laughter made it hard to be serious. Peace had gotten his hands on his other dad's sewing machine, and he'd stitched himself to yards of colorful fabric. The boy was on the run with a tapestry waving behind him like a flag or a cape.

Rage and Gunner were in their usual posts on either side of Mal as he played. Their skinny arms crossed over their chest as if they dared someone to take the toys Mal was playing with. Sometimes he thought it weird how protective they were of Mal, but to be honest, the Crews were a protective group. Sawyer, the twins younger brother, was off by himself with Craig—Linus, Wren, and Hunter's adopted son—hovering nearby. Craig was quiet and a bit on the shy side. The Crews were building a bond stronger than anything blood could ever come close to producing.

The partners hovered over their kids, yet gave them all freedom to be themselves—find their own ways in the world—even from an early age.

The oldest of the group was Juvie at twenty and Princess at fourteen. Even a lot older than their cousins, they never missed a chance to hang out. They were attentive to their cousins, yet tended to hover near each other. They'd become best friends the day Juvie was introduced.

It still amazed him the tight-knit group he'd become a member of in recent years.

"What's with the scowl?" Twitch bounced up beside him and sat down in the lawn chair next to his.

"I didn't know I was scowling."

"Well, you are. So what's the deal? No, wait," Twitch ordered, then called over the rest of the partners.

"Am I about to get a Crew Intervention?"

"Do you think you need an intervention, Uncle Linc," Juvie asked as she stepped up onto the picnic table bench and sat down.

Princess took a seat on the bench and leaned against Juvie's leg.

"No, I definitely don't. There's no reason for it."

"You've been drooling over a certain hot, hairy lead singer for, oh, how long now?" Ben asked with a smirk.

Sometimes he hated that man. Thankfully, Priest was quiet when he joined the group. Priest was quieter and more reserved than the rest, while Priest's husband didn't know what not to say. They were an odd combination, yet they somehow worked perfectly.

Elijah slid a chair closer to him, and he groaned because the man was almost as bad a menace as Twitch.

"Three years, I believe, Twitch, three long and sexually frustrated years."

"Thanks, Eli."

"You're welcome."

The smug grin on the man's too handsome face irked him.

"How the hell does everyone know my business?"

"That's easy. You don't have a poker face." Twitch bounced a bit in the chair. "When King is on stage, you drool, man, drool."

Twitch drew the word out several syllables, and he couldn't help but smile at the man's exuberance. Twitch was always so bubbly, and it was nice to see a man who'd faced what Twitch had and still possess hope.

"I don't do something as undignified as drool."

"Then you've never done a blowjob right."

He jerked his head around to find a serious expression on Elijah's face. The man had to be a sociopath.

"We're out," Juvie announced and dragged Princess away.

"Now, you've scared off the children."

"No, we didn't. My daughter is a lesbian, she's not really into the whole dick thing, and Princess' favorite person is Lily. We're not saying anything they haven't heard from Lily."

Lucky's mother was worse than her son, Lucky. Who the hell raised children in a Radical Honesty household? It seemed too—weird.

"So, since we've found out your blowjob skills are lacking, is it the sex? Do you need advice? We're all friends here, just ask."

"What the hell is going on? Brody and I were sent 9-1-1 texts."

He looked over his shoulder to find Landon and Brody.

"Nothing is going on."

"Of course there is! You need the D, and King has a fine one for ya."

"Has everyone seen King's dick?" He glanced around the group and saw everyone's head nodding a yes.

"That's so cute," Landon said and plopped down on his lap.

The man's lack of knowledge when it came to personal space made him highly uncomfortable. A slender arm came around his shoulders, and he groaned.

"Don't be all jealous. If you'd gone to the lake when we've invited you, you'd have seen it too. So, what's going on here?"

"Intervention," Twitch squealed.

"Oh, we haven't had one of those since Ben."

Brody leaned down and kissed his cheek. "Just take it, Linc, they won't let you escape. Landon is like Wonder Woman's Lasso of Truth, but he sits on you until you talk." The man straightened and barely braced himself before Princess was hugging him, then taking off again to watch over the kids.

"What have we learned?" Landon asked.

"We've learned that Linc has terrible—"

"My blowjob skills are exemplary." His face flamed as his voice rose a bit too much and Juvie barked out a loud laugh nearly tripping as they played Keep Away with Mal as the prize. "I hate you all."

"No, you don't, you love us. You know why?" Elijah kicked his ankle.

"Oh, wise one, why is that?"

"Because we're fucking awesome. The best friends a person could have, and we give the best advice. You have met our husbands, right?"

He answered Elijah, "Definitely."

"Each one is an asshole, moody, violent, sexy as fuck, possessive and love us unconditionally. Being a Crew husband isn't the easiest gig around."

"No, it's not. Crave gets all growly and punchy when a man pays too much attention. He's so cute," Twitch said.

"You calling Crave cute is disturbing. Your husband is a beast."

Crave was like the Incredible Hulk, he had muscles on top of muscles, and the bastard had an eight-pack. No normal man has one of those, and it earned Crave more shriveled dick steroid jokes than he could count since he'd started hanging out with the crews.

"A very sexy and sweet beast, at least to me. So, what's holding you back from making your feelings known?"

"How about the whole ex-brother-in-law thing?"

"Is it because his dick was in your sister that freaks you out?"

Priest channeled Lucky, and that was scary.

"Wouldn't it freak y'all out if you hooked up with your husband's sibling?"

"We see where you're coming from, Linc, but are you going to throw away something that could make you happy just because of an insignificant issue?" Brody piped up.

"The man I want was married to my sister."

Landon sucked his teeth and let out a heaving sigh. "We can't worry about every person our husbands' hooked up with before us. What do you want more, to watch the man you love hook up with someone else or get him for yourself?"

Landon always hit below the belt. Elijah and him knew where to hit to make it hurt when someone was being stupid. He hadn't anticipated developing feelings for King. The attraction was instant. The man was a beast—huge and hairy—it hit all his attraction triggers. What he felt seemed right, but also wrong at the same time. What was he going to do if it all blew up and he lost everything he'd ever wanted?

"You can't drown yourself in guilt. Being attracted to someone isn't really up to us. When I saw Scary the first time, oh, fuck, you should've been inside my head. He looked mean and acted like he hated me, but I instantly gravitated toward him. Even though I was nervous, I felt safe with him around and then I met Tank. I didn't see the scars or mind his silence…to me he was perfect. They treat me and each other like we're the best things to ever happen in their lives. Do you really want to throw aside that because you're feeling guilty?"

"How about talking to Melanie? You two are close, best friends. Maybe discuss it before saying no." Landon gave him a hug and laid his cheek on the top of his head.

"I think he should pounce on King when he gets home," Twitch suggested. "Or tie him to the bed and don't let him up until he's begging."

"Crave lets you tie him up? Wow, your sexy Daddy has secrets." Landon grinned as he winked at Twitch.

"He likes to make me happy."

"Anyone within a mile of where you two are fucking knows how happy he makes you."

He blocked out the conversation and let his mind wander to the pouncing part and away from a bound Crave. How many times over the years had he fantasized about King? The powerful work-hardened muscles. The tanned hair-roughened skin. The way the man filled out a t-shirt and a pair of jeans, or the times he'd seen King in nothing but briefs. His thick bush peeking over the waistband.

"Down, boy, you're not my type."

"Shut up."

Landon laughed, and the rest joined in. Sometimes he loved having them as friends, and other times like this, he didn't understand why he hung out with them.

"You're so sensitive, a sure sign of sexual frustration. So, since you're going to be an idiot, we're going to tell you what to do."

"Is that right, Landon? And what is it that I should do?"

"Claim your fucking man. Life is too fucking short. If we all went with first impressions, most of us wouldn't be happily married with families. You're being a dick. King wants you too. You may be blind as fuck, but none of the rest of us are. Do yourself a favor and get your man before someone else snatches up King and you got to watch him get all lovey and dirty with someone else."

Landon smacked a kiss on his cheek and stood. Everyone but Twitch wandered back to their posts watching the kids play.

"Crave loves me, me. He's kissed every scar and told me he loved me. I ran too long because I didn't think I was worthy."

He turned to watch Twitch stare off into the distance as he spoke.

"I get to wake up to a man who doesn't judge me for all the times I thought I was weak and needed to take a razor to my skin. Doesn't look down on me when I need a little more affection on certain days. He just holds me tighter. He makes everything calm. Don't you want that? Someone to make it calm? To be there to hold you up when you think you're going to fall or celebrate your accomplishments?"

His heart broke for Twitch. He'd heard the stories. Seen the anxiety that sometimes held the tiny man in a choke hold and the instant relief when Crave simply touched him. Since he'd met the Crews, he witnessed countless times the absolute and unconditional love that existed between the partners. It was beautiful and jealousy-inducing.

"I just don't know how, Twitch." He lifted his hand to scratch his beard.

"Falling in love is never easy. It's not supposed to be. But if we don't give it a chance, we lose the opportunity for something great."

"What if I lose him and Mal?"

"I doubt you will. If I know anything, from a lot of years of observation, King is as twisted up in the head as you. Grab it while you can. King is a great guy, and he's going to make some man a lucky partner one day."

Twitch left him with that and took off in pursuit of Peace who was still running around with the sari flying behind him. Suddenly being alone, it all crashed down on him. The possibility of losing King and Mal to someone else—someone else loving King and some other man being Mal's dad. Could he handle that? The answer was no.

He needed to set aside a decade of guilt, and that was going to be harder than anything he'd ever done in his life.

7 Broken Bones and Heavy Meds

King felt like he'd drank way too much the night before and was still drunk as he woke. He groaned as he tried to sit up and his head spun. "Shit, what the fuck did I..." He stopped talking as he glanced around. *Hospital room.* The last thing he remembered was getting back to the garage last night to drop off his truck for the weekend.

"You will never do that shit to me again." Linc's pissed off voice took him by surprise.

He jerked his gaze to the door and instantly regretted it as his stomach turned over onto itself.

"What the hell happened?"

He flopped back onto the bed and raised his hands to cover his eyes. He tried to remember. Did he hit his head?

"You decided to help out in the garage last night before coming home. Brakes failed on a rig coming in, and you jumped to get out of the way and rolled against a stack of barrels. They came crashing down and hit just right, breaking your leg in two places."

"How bad?"

"Luckily clean breaks didn't require surgery, but you're sidelined for a while."

"Shit, what am I supposed to do—"

"Your boss said your benefits will cover bills and all until you're back at work."

"Why do I feel drunk?"

"They got you on the good meds."

"Where's Mal?"

"He's crashing with Mary."

"Mary?"

How fucking hard did he hit his head?

"Yes, Mary. I called everyone I could, but Bear is at some convention, and Joker and Dem are out at the shack for their anniversary. Brawlers Crew is all-hands-on-deck. Twirled Crew are also away at some convention. Lily and Damon were a bit…indisposed. Harper and Ghost went to Atlanta to see Lou and for a prenatal appointment. And Sin and Saint went to see their mother because she needed Saint to act as pilot for a survivalist weekend. The guy that was supposed to do it got food poisoning."

"Was she okay—"

Linc waved off his question. "She was great. When I left Mal, her and Killer were curled up on the couch watching cartoons and eating popcorn."

"Okay, I know Mary—"

"Mary is fine, and I think her and Bear have something going."

"Really?" The more he tried to think, the more his head pounded. He had to be having some fucked up dream—a parallel universe type shit.

"Yep. Because if I'm not mistaken, she was wearing one of Bear's favorite t-shirts."

"He hasn't—"

Bear told him everything. The man was more than his uncle; Bear became one of his best friends.

"Let them have their privacy."

"How long before I get out of here?"

"They want to keep you for a few days until the swelling goes down and they can cast your leg."

"I'm sorry."

"For what?"

"I was going to take you to dinner tomorrow night and let you get some—"

"I don't need alone time, King, I love spending time with Mal and you. I thought about it, and I'd like the guest room, but we'll talk about that later. Right now, you're going to get some rest."

"Is Melanie coming home?"

"Not until next weekend. I sent her a bus ticket. Get some sleep."

"Thanks, honey."

He reached for Linc's hand, laced their fingers and pulled the man down. He groaned as Linc's weight landed on his chest. Linc's forearms were braced on the bed beside his head. Fuck, Linc was beautiful to him, the weight of him perfect, and heavy meds be damned, his body responded. He'd only meant to give him a hug, take advantage of a moment of selfishness, but it turned into something else. Linc's eyes were wide, and his full lips parted.

There was no time to think, just one kiss, it was all he'd take. He tilted his head and curved his right hand around the back of Linc's neck. The anticipation built in the microseconds until he brought their mouths together. He groaned at the softness of Linc's lips; the coarseness of his man's beard and Linc was his. Linc stiffened against him, and he didn't want to give Linc the chance to pull away.

He flicked his tongue along the tight seam of Linc's lips. He tasted Linc's soft gasp. Savored the way Linc settled his weight heavier on him. He kept their fingers linked as he moved his arm around Linc's waist and pinned Linc's right hand at the base of the man's back.

He slowly seduced a response from Linc. Soft brushes, sharp nips, and gentle sucks at the supple curves of Linc's lips. He groaned deeply as Linc opened and he deepened the kiss, teased his tongue over Linc's. And then Linc was his, the kiss intensified—roughened, and the sounds Linc made became higher and needier. Linc's fingers played with his hair. Short nails scored his scalp.

That's his man, sweet and loving. His high feeling bloomed and had nothing to do with the meds. Yes, the caress of their lips was desperate and hungry, but it wasn't hurried. They savored the moment. He'd waited years for this and no way would he rush it.

Linc mumbled and tried to pull away.

"Where you going, honey? Stay right where you are," he ordered. He tightened his arm around Linc to keep him in place.

"What are you doing? Your meds—"

"Nothing to do with meds, nothing at all. So sexy. Soft. You want me, don't deny it, please."

He shifted and drew attention to their hard cocks trapped between them. Linc's was trapped behind denim, but he didn't have that luxury. The thin gown didn't hide the thickness of his dick pushing into the softness of Linc's stomach.

"We can't. What happens…"

They exchanged small kisses as they spoke. Linc's eyes were heavy-lidded and blissed out. He wondered if the man would have the same expression when he was deep inside Linc or Linc balls deep in him. Either way, he couldn't wait to find out.

"You said yes to our date."

"I thought it was a thank you dinner."

"Date. We might have to wait until...shit." He hissed as his leg suddenly made its condition known.

"Oh shit, fuck, I have to get—"

He didn't fight Linc's retreat. The pain quickly grew to excruciating, and his hard-on was only a pleasant memory. He couldn't even bring himself to half-heartedly tease Linc about his out of character cursing.

"I'll get the nurse...just hold on."

Linc was gone, and agony caused his stomach to turn again. He wouldn't puke, he wouldn't—he took deep breaths and tried to focus on their first kiss and nothing else.

Two days and they finally sprung him from the hospital. He was glad to be home, but Linc was skittish. The man refused to look at him. Linc kept busy with Mal and getting everything ready for when Melanie came home. He felt as if he'd fucked up. The kiss they shared had nothing to do with meds or pain, he'd tried to explain, but Linc couldn't get away from him fast enough.

He wanted it all, Linc as his partner and husband. Sharing a life raising Mal together like they'd always done. Maybe he'd made a mistake. The kiss had taken Linc by surprise, and he'd been under the effect of painkillers.

Linc had taken Mal to the store for groceries. When he needed advice, he called two people—Melanie or Bear. Melanie would throw around a lot of I told you sos, so he called Bear instead.

"How ya doing, son?"

King snorted, the man was barely a decade older, but always called him son.

"I can barely get around, and Linc and Mal abandoned me."

"Linc called and said he was going to the grocery store and asked me did I need anything. So I doubt he abandoned your ass."

"I kissed him."

"Finally got your shit together. So, you a couple now?"

"He's avoiding me."

"You're in the same house, that's almost impossible."

"It's possible." *Linc Didn't Want to be Alone with King*

Fuck, fuck, fuck! He pretended to be busy cleaning the kitchen and refrained from calling Bear to tell the man to bring Mal back. It was childish and a bit cowardly, and he understood that. But he didn't want to be alone with King. The kiss was a mistake. King had been drugged. Otherwise, there was no way King would have kissed him. He gripped the plate under the water until the blunt edges cut into his hands.

He tensed as he sensed the moment King entered the room. No matter where they were or how crowded it was, he always knew when King was there.

"You going to keep avoiding me?"

He rolled his lips between his teeth and hung his head. Moment of truth. He removed his hands from the water and grabbed the towel to dry them, then he turned around.

"I don't want to hear the kiss was a mistake, even if it was."

"Who the fuck said it was a mistake?" Genuine confusion thickened King's tone.

"It had to be, you were—"

"If you say I was high, we're going to have our first fight."

Oh, he hated fighting, and he didn't like King mad. The man grew quiet and pulled into himself. Confrontation wasn't something either of them dealt with easily.

"But—"

He observed King as the man leaned against the wall heavily. King was beyond handsome, and as much as he'd fantasized about King over the years, he'd never anticipated being in this situation.

"But nothing, baby. This is between you and me."

"What about Melanie? What would—"

King cut him off, and the man smiled.

"She's known for a long time."

"She would've told me. That isn't something she'd keep from me."

He and Melanie shared everything. She'd been the first he'd told when he'd come out. She knew every crush—well, not everyone—and secret.

"I didn't want her to."

"Why?"

"You remember the first time we met?"

"Yes, I just moved back to town, you were at the parent's house cutting the grass for them."

He could never forget that day. It was the first time he'd ever experienced actual guilt. He'd lusted after his sister's boyfriend. For years, he'd pictured King as his and wondered what belonging to King would be like, even when he knew it was impossible. If King was telling the truth, then he could have a chance at everything he wanted.

"I thought you were the most beautiful man I'd ever seen. Do you know how guilty I felt? There's Melanie, and all I could think about was kissing her brother. It was so fucked up, or from the view inside my closet, it was fucked up. I was such a hypocrite. I always knew Melanie was bi, and she'd accept me, but I was terrified."

"You wanted to kiss me?"

"Every time I saw you, heard your voice, or smelled the scent of your cologne, and everything felt...right. Linc, I didn't plan the kiss at the hospital, didn't realize it until it was happening, but nothing, and I mean nothing, about that kiss was a mistake.

"Did you ever think of me as more than your brother-in-law or ex-brother-in-law?"

He nodded. "I was such an asshole for wanting you. You were dating my sister, married to my sister, and had Mal. I felt like such a bastard the day Mal was born."

"Why?"

"Because I stood in the corner as you and Melanie lay in the hospital bed, cooing over Mal, and I felt so..."

"So what? Just get it out. If we're going to see if this dating thing is going to work, might as well start off with all the cards on the table."

"Jealous. When I held Mal for the first time, he was exactly like you, and he was perfect, beautiful. I wanted to be able to say he was mine."

"Mal is yours."

"Yeah, I'm the uncle."

"No, you're as much a dad as I am. Melanie and me were in complete agreement, over the last three years, Mal has been ours. Yours, mine, and Melanie's, co-parents. It may not seem normal, but you're more than Uncle Lincoln to Mal, or me and Melanie.

"Come here, baby."

He hesitated, but finally got himself moving across the kitchen, one foot in front of the other. He stopped with only a few feet left between them.

"I said, come here."

King grabbed his t-shirt and tugged him close until their chests were pressed together.

"Would you go on a date with me?"

"Really?"

"Yeah, we're gonna do this right. Dating, getting to know each other as Linc and King, not former in-laws."

"We've known each other almost a decade."

"But I'm sure there's a lot we don't know."

"Like what?"

"I'm sure you've kept a few secrets."

Oh, fuck, he didn't want to divulge any of his secrets. That would be so bad.

"No, not really."

"Lying already," King whispered as he leaned in.

His eyes closed as King's breath fanned the side of his throat. He nearly lost his mind as King's calloused hand slipped beneath his shirt and stroked upward until rough fingertips teased his nipple.

"Now, there's something I didn't know."

"What?"

King pinched the small hardened peak, and he bit his lip. He wasn't ready for it, but he arched his back. His nipples were embarrassingly sensitive, always had been.

"How sensitive your nipples are."

"I thought we were going to date."

He tried to distract King, but when King slipped his hands from under his shirt, he nearly whimpered at the loss. Too much time had passed since someone had touched him—since he'd gotten laid. He didn't want to think about how long. The closest thing he got to sex nowadays was imagining King fucking him rough as he stroked one out before he went to sleep. His sex life hadn't been the greatest over the years, but abstinence was hell.

"We are, but I couldn't resist." King's stroked his lips up to his ear. "I've waited a long fucking time to be able to do this. Forgive my lack of control."

He tilted his head back as King nipped at his earlobe, then sucked and bit.

"We're not going to do any more than this until at least after the first date."

"Are we going to make it to the first date?"

He felt King's smile against his skin and loved that he'd put it there. Making King happy always brightened his mood. King had the biggest smile, and it deepened the sexy crinkles at the corners of his eyes. He'd watched King change from a baby-faced twenty-year-old to a sexy, mature man with laugh lines and a few silver strands in his dark hair.

"Yes, yes we are. Now, behave. I'm wounded, and you're taking advantage."

He gently pushed King away and looked into King's shimmering gaze. King couldn't hide his emotions because it was always right there for everyone to see. Well, he apparently hid his interest well, and he wondered how he had missed it.

"I'm taking advantage. Did you double your meds?"

"No, but only because I haven't taken them."

King liked to push himself a little too much, and he was going to have to watch the man a little closer. King wasn't the type to sit around. He worked hard during the week, came home and took care of Mal, then played in his band. King was never still.

"Shit, you need to take them and rest."

"You've been cussing an awful lot lately. Have you been hanging out with the crews again?"

"I went and had drinks with Livingston, Pure and Little."

"Why? Was it like a double date?"

He nearly snorted at what he assumed was a touch of jealousy. That was new.

"No, not a double date, nowhere near. I think Little had a date, they didn't show, he called Livingston and Pure. I was there picking up dinner."

"Little has the worst luck with dates."

"I feel bad for him. On the one hand, he's a bit crazy and outlandish, but he's a nice guy."

"True, I don't think he's made it through a date in the past year. Lily said she's been tracking him down at his place when she finds out."

"Lily and Little as best friends is a bit weird. And he has a place?"

Little, as far as he knew, stayed at Lily and Damon's a few nights a week and kept a plentiful stash of clothes in his surveillance van. No one knew much about Little. They knew him now, but his past seemed off-limits for conversation. He suddenly felt ashamed he hadn't made more of an effort with Little.

"No one really knows where. His paranoia is legendary, but Mal loves him."

"They love their fun Uncle Little. I just won't take him to the playground again."

"What did he do?"

"Got stuck in the tube. He had three kids trying to push him through, and all he was doing was laughing his butt off."

King laughed and shook his head.

"Let's get you back to bed. You shouldn't be up and standing for so long."

"Yes, dear."

He rolled his eyes as he helped King turn and he walked behind him as the man maneuvered the crutches. It was a slow pace, but he enjoyed the play of King's powerful muscles beneath the cotton of his t-shirt. The man was built like Bear with bulky muscles, but he didn't have the man's height.

"When is Bear bringing Mal back?"

"Before he opens the shop tomorrow. Oh, Bear and Mary are dating."

"Like we didn't see that one coming," he quipped as he helped King back into bed.

He took the crutches and placed them against the wall beside the nightstand.

"Tomorrow I make dinner…we'll have our date."

"No, I'll make dinner. You're not standing up that long."

"Yes, dear."

"Don't yes, dear me. I know you remember, you can't be on the go all the time. You have to heal. Don't mess your leg up worse than it already is."

He opened King's pill bottle, shook out two, and handed them to him along with a bottle of water. He waited to make sure the man took them. King was sneaky, and when he was sick, he was even sneakier.

"I'll do as you say, on one condition."

"And what would that be?"

"Sleep with me."

"I don't—"

"Don't think, just change your clothes and lie down with me."

"Okay, but don't be trying anything."

"With my leg, I can't be loving on you the way I want, so next best thing is you can sleep beside me."

"I'll be right back."

He hurried through finishing the dishes and making sure the house was locked up, but on his way back to King's room, he hesitated. He stood in the middle of the hallway.

This was happening. King wanted him, and Melanie wasn't going to hate him or stop talking to him. He'd already lost his parents, so he couldn't lose Melanie, Mal, or King. They were the only family he had. His parents ignored his coming out, pretended he was going to find some woman someday, then get married and have kids. He wanted to get married and have kids. He just wanted to do it with the man he loved. He wouldn't lose his family over this—he still had them. He stood a bit taller. He could do this.

He entered King's room, grabbed pajamas from King's dresser like always and headed to the bathroom to change. He glanced at King to find the man stretched out, his arms folded under his head, and King watched every move he made. He could get used to that, but first, King owed him a first date. He couldn't wait.

8 Be a Gentleman, King, Be a Motherfucking Gentleman

Be a fucking gentleman, King warned himself as he pretended to be relaxed—until Linc disappeared into the bathroom. Did he have time to call Melanie? No, no, she'd laugh her ass off at him. Bear would be all calm and logical, and just piss him off.

He could do this, he shifted his leg on the pillow, then lifted his hands to scrub his face and rub his eyes. He focused on the sounds of Linc getting ready for bed.

Over the years, he'd lost count of how many times he had imagined that; in bed waiting for his man to join him. Those nights hadn't involved a broken leg and pain meds. He wasn't going to complain, though.

He slipped his arms back under his head as the bathroom door opened and he turned to watch Linc exit. A groan rumbled up from his chest as a shirtless Linc strode around the bed. The dark, blond hair on the man's chest wasn't as thick as his own, but it covered the man from collarbones to the waist of the pajama pants. Linc's rounded belly was perfect, and he wanted to nuzzle the hairy curve, then head lower.

"What are you thinking about?"

"How fucking sexy you are."

Linc's face turned red, but the man attempted to hide it by bending over to pull down the covers.

"You are. I've always thought so."

He waited until Linc had lain down and turned toward him. Linc avoided looking at him. He wasn't going to let that happen.

"Come here." He shifted and slipped his arm beneath Linc's head, tugged Linc to his side. His dick hardened at the weight of Linc's thick frame along his.

Not the time, he warned himself.

Linc rested his arm across his stomach and tucked his head beneath King's chin.

King turned to press a kiss to the man's forehead.

"You okay," Linc asked.

"Yes, I'm fine. I took my meds. I'll be asleep in no time."

"What's Melanie going to think about this?"

He ran his fingers through Linc's soft hair and closed his eyes to inhale the lemon scent of Linc's shampoo.

"She'll tell me I finally got my head out of my ass. She's known for a long time."

"And still, she never told me."

"What would you've said if she had?" he asked as he tugged and tilted Linc's head back. He studied the hazel flecks in Linc's blue-green eyes. As Linc closed his lids, the long pale lashes fanned his high cheekbones. He placed his left hand on Linc's face and stroked his thumb along the fringe of those lashes. "What would you have done?"

"Denied it."

An edge of sadness tinged Linc's words.

He lowered his head to brush his mouth to Linc's, and the man's lips trembled under his. For so long, he'd imagined being able to hold and kiss Linc that the reality paled in comparison to the dream. Linc shifted and raised his chin. He deepened the kiss, and their breathing rough and moans echoed, coming in sync. He pulled Linc on top of him—the man's weight bearing him down into the mattress and he wanted more.

He knew it couldn't go beyond a make-out session, but he wanted it to be more than about the physical. Fuck it; talking could come later. He wrapped his hand around Linc's thigh and muscled the man on top of him. Linc straddled him.

"You're not getting in my pants. You know that right?"

Linc smiled against his lips. "Who said I wanted in your pants?"

"At least we got that cleared up."

He splayed his hands over Linc's shoulder blades and stroked downward. His fingers dipped into the hollow of Linc's spine until he reached the waistband of Linc's pants. He slipped his fingers beneath the soft cotton and cupped Linc's fuzzy cheeks. He kneaded the thick muscles.

"Hey, what about not getting into pants?"

"Honey, I said my pants, I didn't say anything about yours."

"I think turnabout is fair play, right?"

He opened his mouth to make a comment, but nothing came out as strong fingers pushed into his loose gym shorts. His back arched and his body tensed as Linc wrapped his hand around his dick.

"This isn't what I had in mind." He pushed the statement through clenched teeth.

Linc stroked lower until he had his balls cupped in his palm. He gripped Linc's hips tightly.

"I swore I was going to be—"

He let out a string of curses as Linc pushed his hand between his thighs. He shifted them as far apart as Linc's legs allowed.

"Ten years I've waited to get my hands on you. All the time you were with Melanie, then all the men I had to watch flirt with you…get to go home with you. Jealous, so fucking jealous."

"Is that all you want…to get your hands on me?"

He knew what everyone thought about him. That he was only a flirt and fuck. They didn't understand how badly he wanted Linc and not having him killed something inside him.

"Look at me," Linc ordered.

He almost ignored it until the man's hand disappeared and came up to grip his chin. Firm, full lips stroked over his face, teased the corners of his mouth and he met the man's gaze.

"No, it's not all I want. I want the dates…" Another kiss. "And everything that goes along with it."

He almost protested when Linc moved to the side to lay down beside him.

"Turn over," Linc said as he nudged his hip.

He carefully turned to his side and became the little spoon when Linc pressed against his back.

Linc slipped his arm under his head and banded his other across his chest until his hand hooked under his arm.

"I've never felt quite good enough. I'm fat and hairy, past my prime."

"Bullshit."

Linc nipped the side of his neck with just enough force to make it sting. He turned his head giving Linc more access. He closed his eyes as Linc stroked his chest, teased his nipples with slightly roughened fingertips, then over his stomach. He held his breath as Linc worked his shorts down his hips. The air in the room was cool against his exposed hip and groin.

"Let me finish."

"Yes, sir."

"Good boy."

He snorted, and Linc squeezed him tighter. Linc's fingers played in his thick pubes. His cock was hard and aching. He wanted Linc's touch there. The man's firm grip. He didn't feel like himself. Any other time he'd grab Linc's hand and put it where he wanted it. Reach around and bring his hand to the thick ridge of dick notched between his cheeks. His shyness was strange but exhilarating. He didn't have to be on, didn't have to pretend to be happy because he was. Content to lie there and let Linc love on and touch him.

Yes, he wouldn't lie. He'd thought about fucking and being fucked by Linc, but he'd also wanted this. Lazy times that built the heat between them until it wasn't enough.

"I've also wanted my brother-in-law turned ex-brother-in-law for a long time knowing or thinking I'd never have a chance.

"You like when I touch you, Andrew?"

He nodded and hummed his affirmative.

"Do you want more?"

He jerked his head in a quick nod.

"Use your words. What do you want?"

"Stroke my dick." His voice broke.

"Like this?" Linc asked.

The rough, quick jacks on his cock caused his fingers to clench in the sheet and pillow. He cursed the stupid cast as his body bowed, and the cumbersome weight restricted his movements. He awkwardly pushed and pulled his dick through Linc's fist.

"So close..." He was so fucking close. He slammed his ass back against Linc's cock. The frightening thickness notched between his cheeks. Bringing his hand back, he gripped Linc's hip as the man rutted.

"Cum, baby," Linc grunted.

The sharp nip to the side of his neck caused him to shout as his balls tightened and he came.

"That was fucking...fuck."

Linc held him so tight it was hard to breathe as the wetness spread across his lower back.

His head felt heavy, and his brain was fuzzy and fried. Between the orgasm and medicine, his energy was tapped out. He turned his head and searched for Linc's mouth, and when they kissed, it was lazy and almost chaste.

"I think we're doing this dating thing backward."

"Don't care." And he didn't. Except for the broken leg, there wasn't anything about that he would change.

"Go to sleep. I'll clean us up."

He grumbled his protests, but he was too weak to move. Closing his eyes, he tried to focus on the sounds of Linc moving around, water running, and then everything faded as he fell asleep.

9 What Now?

What the hell am I going to do now, Linc silently asked himself as he packed up his apartment. He'd given his notice before things had taken a turn with King. Did he regret it—no. Would he do it again—that was the question he couldn't answer. Their first kiss had been in the hospital with King on painkillers. The first time they were intimate, again King had been on painkillers.

He knew he was over thinking the issue, he knew, but that didn't change the fact he was doing it. Men like him just didn't get the bad boy that was only good for their man. He wasn't like his friends Twitch, Gregory, Ben, Elijah, the list of could go on. Their men were scary as fuck—the quintessential bad boys.

"You're doing it." Melanie's tone was accusatory.

"Doing what?" he asked as he shoved more books into the box.

"Questioning shit. You can't tell me something didn't happen between you and King. It was written on his face when he leaned in to kiss you, and you avoided it."

Not his proudest moment, but he'd felt uncomfortable with Melanie in the room with them. He'd seen the hurt in King's beautiful eyes. In all the time he'd known King, he'd only seen the man have that look when King's parents rejected him.

"I didn't mean to hurt him."

"But you did, and you have to apologize, soothe that man's feelings."

"I'm just worried about what you—"

"Oh, fuck, no, this doesn't have anything to do with me. King and me are divorced. Except for being co-parents and best friends, there's nothing between us anymore. I don't even know if there ever was."

He turned and sat down on his couch to study Melanie.

"What do you mean?"

She shuffled across the room and plopped down next to him.

"We were in this sort of best friend's clusterfuck. Always together. When we were sixteen, everyone was having sex and, oh, fuck, was that drunken first time awkward. There was barely any eye contact for almost a week afterward."

"You two just seemed so right together."

"That's because we were best friends. We knew each other better than we even knew ourselves. Like I said before, I knew King was gay before he admitted it. What I'm trying to say is, I'm a non-issue. Don't ruin what you and King could have because you think I'm going to be heartbroken...I'm not."

"But you two have—"

"Oh, we had sex, lots and lots of sweaty, dirty sex. Did I mention the—"

"I know!"

Melanie laughed loudly as she bumped him with her shoulder.

"Let's finish packing up your stuff. The movers will be here soon to take everything but your bedroom furniture to storage. Then you can go home to your man. I'll take Mal out for dinner and leave you and King to do all that mushy stuff."

Melanie stood and started to walk off, he reached for her hand and stopped her.

"Thanks."

"Don't thank me. Just fix what you did, deal?"

He nodded, and once she disappeared, he went back to work. Being the asshole wasn't him, and hurting King wasn't an option, but he had hurt him. He needed to take his man on a date to make up for it.

It was time to move forward since he was a grown ass man of forty. He wasn't some kid who didn't know what they wanted. The dream of King finally turned into reality, and he wasn't going to fuck that up with old insecurities.

He went back to packing quickly so he could get home.

###

The idea of being alone with King had been a good one until Melanie walked out the door with Mal. It felt like he hadn't spent enough time with Mal lately, and also King withdrew from him when he got home earlier to move everything into his new room.

His body ached, and he was so tired, but he needed to make everything right, he couldn't delay. He finger-combed his damp hair and dropped his towel in the hamper as he exited his room. He went in search of King, but it wasn't that hard to find him. The subtle strumming of a guitar and soft singing drew him to the front porch.

He eased the screen door open and lightly stepped outside. King didn't see him or simply ignored his presence. This was one of the times he didn't mind. King killed it at southern rock or heavy metal when he was on stage, but the man could sing and play *Otis Redding's These Arms of Mine* like no one else.

Crossing his arms, he leaned against the wood siding of the cabin and just listened, watching King's fingers work over the strings. It had been months since he'd been treated to a private show. The deep bass of King's voice caused a chill to move over his skin. So many times over the years, he'd pretended King sang the songs only for him. The man could make the blues sound downright erotic when King took a break from the rough and growling metal.

The music faded out, and he felt the loss soul deep. He remained quiet in case he was lucky enough to get another song but it didn't happen.

"I'm sorry."

"For what?" King asked without looking at him.

"You know damn well what."

"Everyone has considered me a flirt and a fuck for so long, I just…"

"I know what you thought, and it had nothing to do with that. It was all me. You have to understand how weird it is to be affectionate when Melanie walks into the room."

"We talked about this, Melanie told me you two talked."

He rolled his lips between his teeth and sighed heavily through his nose. "I know, but it didn't prepare me for when she walked into the kitchen. I'm sorry I was an idiot."

King lifted his guitar off his lap and leaned it on the wall. "Come here," King said and patted his lap.

"I'm too—"

"Shut the fuck up and come here."

He rolled his eyes and strode across the short expanse between them and turned, then lowered himself carefully to King's lap. The edge of the cast cut into his right thigh and ass cheek.

"Now, isn't that better?"

"If you're in that cast longer because you have me sitting on your lap, that's on you."

"You're such a pain in the ass."

The crunch of gravel under heavy tires caused him to squint at the headlights approaching. He started to get up, but King stopped him by wrapping his arms around his waist.

"I'm not interrupting, am I?"

He smiled at Livingston Francis' voice. The large man was Linus Trenton's right-hand man at Trenton Security. The dim porch lights highlighted the planes and dips of the severe scarring that covered the man's right side. Strangely, it didn't take away from the handsomeness of Liv. Liv had that dangerous edge that would draw men and women to the bad boy image. Sad thing the man was a complete asshole, but most of the guys who worked for Trenton were.

"No, what are you doing out here?" King asked.

"I'm hiding from Little."

"What did Little do now," he inquired, and part of him was frightened to find out.

The Trenton Security Crew had integrated easily into the dynamic of Twirled, Brawlers, and Executioners Crews over the last few years. They were an odd crew.

"He locked Pure and Raul in the weapons cage overnight with condoms and lube. Said he wasn't letting them out until they fucked."

King laughed loudly.

A smile played at the edges of his mouth at Liv's disgusted tone.

"Why are you hiding? It seems more like Little is the one in trouble," he asked.

"Oh, he is. But he snuck into the backseat of my vehicle, and I was halfway home before I realized. I put him out."

"Raul in jail yet?"

Raul was an intense guy. Quick to fight and uber protective of Pure which was weird since Pure was taller than Raul and fifty pounds heavier. Pure's marksman skills were legendary, and he'd heard Pure was a SWAT sniper before he'd come to work for Linus.

"No, but Pure was embarrassed as fuck, and that pissed Raul off and, well—"

"He's out for blood," King supplied.

"Yeah. This a new development." Liv nodded toward them.

He sighed. "Extremely new."

"About fucking time. You two been dancing around each other for as long as I've known y'all. King's been waiting for you to smarten up?"

"Did everyone know but me?"

"Pretty much."

Was he that clueless, so oblivious about King's attraction that he hadn't seen it for years...apparently, he was. He glanced at King as the man's fingertips danced over his rounded stomach and his right love handle. The urge to suck in his stomach hit him, but he tried to dispel the urge.

King straightened and pressed firm lips to his ear, then whispered, "I know what you just did, and I didn't like it."

When King relaxed back in the chair, he started to protest but bit his tongue.

"You want a beer?"

"No, man, I'm good, just trying to get Little off my tail. Someone needs to put a leash on that boy."

With the way Liv had said that, he was positive Liv meant an actual leash. He'd heard stories about some of the Trenton Crew and some had quite a few kink fetishes. When Liv was asked about finding someone, the man only replied with he didn't have the time or energy to find his boy.

King laughed. "He can't get through one date before they start running."

"Ain't that the fucking truth. Lily doesn't help. She enables his crazy."

He protested, "He's fine. Little will meet someone when he's ready."

"Not if Raul disposes of his body before Little gets the chance."

"Well, Pure is a little clueless about Raul's interest."

"Raul hasn't even asked Pure out." Liv's tone deepened with disgust.

"Linc, Raul ain't gonna ask Pure out. Pure can't run away fast enough."

He'd watched Raul and Pure together when they were all at Brawlers. Pure kept so much distance between Raul and himself that it was noticeable. He wondered what Pure had against the man, but Pure didn't seem to pay attention to anyone. The rumors were Pure had that nickname for a reason, but he couldn't imagine a man that handsome made it to almost thirty without being touched.

King's chuckle pulled him from his thoughts.

"How did they get out of the cage?"

"Linus and Pelter had a meeting about a new operation."

"Shit," King said and shook his head.

"Yep, Pelter threatened a false imprisonment charge, and Little ran…"

"Right into the backseat of your SUV."

"I think Little's van will make it onto a roof before morning. I better get going to let you two have your privacy. I just needed to hide out for a few. Let me know when your next gig at Brawlers is. I don't want to miss it."

"I will, thanks, man, come by anytime."

Liv didn't say anything else, just waved and turned to disappear back into the darkness.

Suddenly, he was pulled down onto King's chest.

"Are we good?" King asked.

"Yeah, we're good. I really am sorry. I'm just not used to all this and part of me is waiting—"

"For me and Melanie to freak out about you and me being together…don't. We've talked about it for years. It may feel weird, but it isn't. We'll just take it one step at a time, okay?"

"Okay. You want dinner?"

"No, I just want to sit here with you for a bit."

He smiled to himself as he laid his head on King's shoulder and kissed the man's rough cheek. He inhaled the scent of King and drew it deep into his lungs. If there was one thing he was sure of, the relationship between them wouldn't be easy. There was a lot they hadn't worked out. But for the time being, he was happy and hoped he stayed that way.

10 Blue Balls were Hell

He was going to get carpal tunnel if he jerked off one more fucking time, but each masturbation session was less enjoyable than the last. Dating Linc was his dream come true. He wasn't going to complain about that. It would be stupid to protest it, yet every time he tried to initiate sex, Linc protested. The fucking cast was cramping his style, and it didn't help it itched like a motherfucker. It had already been a month of make-out sessions, and he was about to die. Okay, he was being dramatic, but, fuck, what could one little blowjob hurt?

The fractures were healing well, and the doctor had told them another month and the cast could probably come off. That was not sitting well with him. He was trapped at home and needed a ride to go anywhere. He missed his motorcycle. At least he got to spend time with Mal and Linc; it was great to be home with his family. Melanie had stayed as long as she could before she had to go back to school and work.

He'd told Melanie countless times he'd pay for her to go to school so she wouldn't have to work, just focus on her studies. He would remember that punch until his dying day.

"Daddy," Mal squealed, and he turned to find his son behind him being chased by Rage and Gunner.

Oh man, they took pleasure in making his son scream as they tickled him, but if Mal fell and got a scrape, the twins were devastated.

The air whooshed from his lungs as Mal launched his sturdy little body onto his stomach.

"Give him back," Rage demanded.

Gunner just glared at him. Those two were like mini-versions of Psycho. The man could've had the twins himself; their personalities must be genetic.

"And why should I do that?" he asked as he rubbed his giggling son's back.

The twin heavy sighs amused him and the fact they tipped their heads back like they were counting to ten. A complete Psycho move.

"Where are your dads at?"

"Locked in the bathroom. We need tools."

"And why do you need tools?"

They looked at him like he was an idiot. That's what happened when you named your kids Gunner and Rage.

"To take the da...door apart."

"Rage, you're not taking the door apart, they'll be out in a minute. Now, what were y'all doing to Mal?"

"We made him lunch."

He was terrified now. "What did y'all make him for lunch?"

"We had Pop make it. It's good." Gunner sounded highly offended.

"The hot dogs are white."

Of course, soy dogs. He'd been a bit disturbed when he saw Psycho making them for the twins.

"Maybe Mal wants something else."

"Do you know what they do to animals to make food?" The twins asked, their voices raised with each word.

"No, and Mal doesn't need to know, now, does he? Psycho," he yelled.

"What the fu—what?" Psycho walked into the living room with a very mussed Ben under his arm.

"Soy dogs, really?"

"You carnivores disgust me. Come on, Mal, I'll make you a sandwich." Psycho plucked Mal from his lap, and he barely avoided a foot to the face.

"Pop, give him to us," Rage and Gunner protested as they took off staying close to Psycho's heels.

"Our sons need to learn that not all meat is murder," Ben said with amusement as he plopped down beside King.

Ben's hair was grayer and the lines on his face a bit deeper than when he'd met the other man, yet he hadn't seen a man as happy with his partner. Psycho couldn't stand to not touch Ben when they were together. They were like that couple everyone wanted to be like. And to be honest, he was surrounded by happy couples, and he wanted to be like them.

"It doesn't seem to be harming them in the growth department. They're not much older than Mal, and they're already at least six inches taller."

"We had them tested, their growth kind of concerned us, but look at my husband."

"True. Where's Sawyer?"

"He's down for his nap. It won't last long…the boy doesn't sleep more than two hours. We've tried everything, and the doctors' have no clue what's going on. Enough about my heathens. How're things going with Linc?"

"I don't know, we've done the date thing several times, but he won't—"

"Sex ain't happening?"

"No, and I mean, I don't mind, taking it slow is fine with me, but just tell me."

"You want us to watch Mal for the night? The twins miss their favorite person."

"If it was up to your twins, Mal would move in with y'all."

"Probably true, I've never known three and four-year-olds wanting to talk on the phone as much as them."

"We're definitely going to have to get them their own phones."

"I think it's kind of cute."

He didn't know about the cute part, he loved his nephews, but those two kids could be scary.

"I was serious about taking him for the night."

"It seems Mal has been spending more time away from home since I hurt my leg and Linc and I got together. I don't want him to feel, I don't know, unloved."

"Mal will be great. He's the most well-adjusted kid I've ever met. The Crews' kids stick together. I only offered because sometimes a new relationship takes a little extra. You and Linc spent a long time as brothers-in-law. It's gotta be a huge shift in the dynamic."

"It is. I get why he's nervous, but both me and Melanie have talked about it. How do you make it work with being best friends with Psycho's ex and her wife, co-parenting and all that?"

"It's natural. Bernie, Stacey and I spent a lot of time talking after we met. We wanted kids, but I didn't want to be a weekend or holiday dad, and I didn't want that for Psycho either. So, the three of us discussed the pros and cons of it all, then we told Psycho what we had decided."

"I'm sure that went over well."

"Well, when we piled into bed with him that morning and said we wanted his sperm it didn't go exactly like we planned.

"Think about it, Melanie has no issues and has known for years. You three have done an amazing job with Mal. Hang-ups happen, but you're grown ass people, and miscommunication is for teenagers who don't know what they want."

"You're a little scary."

"My husband is a great influence. So, are we taking Mal to spend the night with his besties or not?"

"Sure, one night."

Ben tipped his head back and yelled, "Boys, Mal's spending the night."

"We'll help him get his stuff," the twins said in unison as they're footfalls echoed on the hardwood floor. A strange scraping sound came from the direction of the front door, and he turned to see Rage and Gunner dragging a suitcase bigger than the both of them.

"What the hell are they doing? Where did they get the suitcase?"

"Gunner, Rage, do not pack all Mal's stuff, boys." Ben surged from the couch to the sound of Psycho laughing. "It's one night, you can't keep him. Dammit, Psy, you're not helping."

Psycho stood with Mal held on his hip as he smiled at his sons. He'd known Psycho for a long time, and Psycho wasn't the smiling and happy sort, but marriage and kids had softened him a bit.

"What? They got a little crush on Mal. It's not the end of the fucking world."

Psycho spun and headed in the direction of the kitchen. Hopefully, to get Mal something other than soy dogs. How the fuck Psycho maintained almost three hundred pounds on vegetables astounded him.

"Don't take the furn—where did they get tools?"

He shook his head and let it fall back onto the couch. He was too old for this shit.

"Why are the twins trying to stuff everything Mal owns into a suitcase?"

He opened his eyes to see Linc standing over him.

"Apparently they think him spending the night means he's moving in?"

"Can you imagine those three as teenagers?"

"No, I don't want to imagine." His son wasn't dating until he was fifty especially if Mal had a thing for crazy vegetarians when he got older.

Linc laughed and leaned down, giving him an upside-down kiss.

"It'll be fine, at least we know they'll take care of him. He's already got his own security detail."

"Great, they already think the Crew kids are crazy enough."

"Could be worse things than the kids being as tight and protective of each other."

"True."

"You eaten yet?"

"No, Psycho made tofu dogs and who knows what else for the kids."

"I'll make you lunch."

"Thanks, I'll come and help."

He grabbed his crutches and used them to help him stand, then he slowly followed behind Linc. He told himself he wouldn't focus on the curves of Linc's ass, but he completely lied. The man could fill out a pair of jeans. His cock jerked inside his sweatpants, and he willed away the hard-on at least until they had the house to themselves.

Another wave of guilt hit him about Mal spending another night away from home.

"Is it bad Mal's going to spend the night away again?" he asked as he stepped into the kitchen behind Linc.

"Stop, it's one night. We'll pick him up tomorrow. He loves spending time with Rage and Gunner, even when they make him eat veggie burgers."

"We need to pack him something for dinner."

Linc chuckled but didn't comment. He just moved around the kitchen gathering the ingredients for dinner. Ten minutes later, Mal ran into the kitchen with Rage and Gunner close behind. Quick hugs and goodbyes, and Psycho and Ben ushered the kids out the door to Ben's van.

Now that he was alone with Linc, he was at a loss for what to do or say. How did he broach the subject of the elephant in the room? If Linc didn't want him anymore, then he needed to know. He was terrified to hear that it was over before it had even started. It was a cowardly move yet he remained silent and just watched Linc.

11 King Needs to Relax

The house was suddenly too quiet without the twins and Mal running around or Psycho and Ben trying to get a quickie while locked in the bathroom. How the hell he'd gotten mixed up in this crazy, he didn't have a clue? He wouldn't complain too much. These people became more of a family than his own, except for his sister. No matter day or night, if he called, any one of them came—no questions asked.

He set the table with plates filled with sandwiches and chips. He bit back a smile at the twin creases between King's heavy brows. The man was going to get a migraine from thinking too hard. He pushed against King's chest and settled sideways on King's thigh of his uninjured leg.

"Spill it," he ordered.

He loved that King didn't complain just wrapped his arms around his waist and held him tight.

"You've been keeping your distance."

"Is that what this is about? King, you were worried I only wanted you for the night. This isn't about just sex. I needed you to know that it wasn't, and I don't want to lose what I've found with you, Mal, the Crews. For me, I thought going slow was the best option."

"Um, the other night we weren't exactly going slow."

"Heat of the moment, it got a bit out of hand."

"Oh, I was definitely in hand."

"Can we get back on point, please?"

"Fine, slow is nice. Other than Melanie, I never did the whole dating thing before."

"I know."

"Don't sound like that."

"I didn't sound like anything. You're becoming offended by nothing. I've had boyfriends before. I even hooked up for randoms in college."

His man was cute as hell when he pouted.

"You're not a virgin. Mal is proof of that."

"Yeah, yeah, whatever, continue."

"You have a broken limb."

"My dick ain't broke. It works just perfect."

"It does, huh?"

"Uh huh, why don't you find out?"

King nuzzled the side of his neck, his beard rough against his skin, and Linc's breath hitched as teeth sharply nipped at his throat. Instant fucking hard-on. A squeak escaped his mouth as his t-shirt was practically ripped up and over his head. King's big, roughened hand curved around the side of his rounded belly. He involuntarily sucked in his stomach—which to be honest never worked.

The sharp edges of Kings' teeth sunk deeper into his neck. He shivered at the mark he knew would remain. He pushed his hip against the thick, hard ridge inside King's loose shorts.

"Now, baby, what did I say about that?"

"What?"

Was he supposed to be able to think? His ass clenched imaging King's dick sinking deep. King's heavy balls slapping his as King reamed him from behind.

"Get up," King ordered with a deep bass growl.

His mind went blank as it reminded him of King's voice when he sang. The dangerous, hard edges made him hard every time.

King's hard grip forced him to his feet.

The sensual fog which gripped his brain only seconds before cleared with a jarring quickness. He attempted to form questions, but his throat seized up as King shoved his shorts under his hairy balls and wrapped his hand around his red-tipped cock. King lazily stroked from base to tip.

"Take off the rest of your fucking clothes...now."

His face heated and his hands shook. King's expression shifted from rage to lust with such speed it made him dizzy just from watching. He kicked off his shoes dropping his jeans and briefs to his ankles, then kicked them aside. His tongue flicked out to moisten his dry lips as he stared at the beads of pre-come sliding down King's wide shaft. His mouth watered with the urge to taste—to roll King's flavor around his mouth.

King's cock was perfect, from the spongy, flared head to the thick base surrounded by black curls. He wanted to sink his face against King's groin and inhale his strong, musky scent.

King's feral growl of a single no stopped his descent to his knees.

"I don't think you deserve this dick...just yet."

King reached down with his free hand and tugged at his balls.

"Fuck, look at you, baby, all that sexiness is mine. But you know, you tried to hide it from me."

"I didn't—"

"You so fucking did, sucking in that stomach. I think that deserves punishment. So, turn around, lean over the table and present me what's mine."

He started to argue but the raising of one thick brow stopped him, and on unsteady legs, he turned. He pushed the plates and glasses to the opposite end of the table. He laid himself on the surface, the wood cool and jarring as his warm skin met the smooth plane. He rested his cheek to soothe the heat of embarrassment. At the sound of chair legs scraping over the floor, he resisted the urge to glance behind him.

His hips jerked and lifted as King's hands palmed his cheeks, massaging and spreading them apart. Then his breath caught at the sting of one smack. He groaned as he rutted against the smooth surface as one strike after another warmed his ass. Fire flared, it was pain and pleasure, no one had ever spanked him before. King didn't speak to him, and he tried to count each one to focus. His cock was hard and aching, leaving wetness on the under curve of his stomach.

The words tripping and falling from his lips shocked him as he begged like a slut for more. Pleaded to be fucked. Begged for King to stop—to never stop. His back arched and his head came back to rest on his shoulders at the suddenness of King's face buried against his ass. King's beard was rough, while his tongue was soft and wet as it licked and probed his hole.

His short nails dug into the table until his knuckles turned white. Pain took the edge off his pleasure as King squeezed his abused cheeks. The grunts and sexy growls had him pushing onto his toes to get closer. He screamed as King's mouth disappeared and the spanking restarted. Harder and sharper, he wanted to jack his cock and come as King doled out punishment.

Then with no warning, all stimuli ceased, and he didn't care about waiting for permission. He straightened and spun around. Sweat glistened at King's temples and in the thick curls covering the man's chest. The sensual curl of the corner of King's mouth. The bastard knew what he'd done.

He glanced down at himself, cock hard and standing at full attention. Beads of pre-come dripped from the slit. His chest moved with his labored breaths and his skin flushed and sweaty.

"Did you learn your lesson?" King asked.

He didn't lift his head. It hit him, he felt sexy knowing King wanted—needed—him.

"C'mere, baby." King took his hand and pulled him forward.

He stumbled a bit, then stood between King's spread thighs. His man was still cock out. It jumped on King's lower abs, leaving pearly drops. He wanted to drop to his knees, lick them up, and finally find out what King felt like on his tongue. Sliding into his throat.

"S'sexy licking them lips, but you don't get it yet."

He opened his mouth to protest, maybe beg, okay, definitely beg, but his head was tugged down. Strong, thick fingers dug into the back of his neck, and he sighed as their mouths met. It was possessive and hungry—denied too long. A decade of need in one kiss. Violently clashing as ragged breaths were pushed and taken through their noses.

"Fuck," King cursed as he jerked his head back. "We need a bed."

He wasn't going to argue.

"This is going to be the unsexiest walk to the bedroom ever. Help me up, baby." King pulled his shorts back up to cover his hard dick.

He brushed King's lips with his, then helped King to his feet and acted as King's crutch. They made the trip in silence, and his nervousness grew. Lost in the moment, he couldn't think about what came after. He was naked and King was still hard, so the man didn't find him unappealing.

"You know something I've always wanted to do with you?" King asked as he stopped them a few steps away from the bedroom.

"What?"

"Dance with you."

He'd imagined it too, enclosed in each other's embrace swaying under the neon lights of Brawlers as the music played and everyone else faded. Tonight, he wanted something different, a more intimate dance. "Then let's dance."

King took an unsteady step forward and another until they entered the dimly lit room. The covers were already turned down.

"Take off my shorts."

Standing in front of King, his hands shook as he eased the silky fabric over King's hips and let the shorts fall to the floor. King's big, rough hands rose to cup his cheeks, and their lips touched. It surpassed all other kisses, even the ones he'd fantasized about. Although slow and tender, every emotion King felt for him was contained in that single touch. It was raw and beautiful. Punctuated by groans and rough whimpers.

He eased King onto the bed, and the kiss turned awkward as he helped King lift his casted leg onto the bed. He broke the kiss and stretched to his full height. He'd stayed there long enough to know the supplies King kept in his nightstand, but he also knew no one else was ever invited into King's bed. That was his place—his right.

He fumbled with the handle as King stroked the monstrously thick girth of his cock. His ass clenched just thinking about the burn and pain, and, oh, how he wanted it. Years had passed, nights of nothing more than toys and his own hand to ease his need.

"Now, you're going to go to your room and get your favorite toy and bring it back here."

"Why?"

"I'm going to watch you get yourself ready for me."

"No—"

"Yes, do as I say."

Oh fuck, King lay on the bed lazily stroking his cock and all he wanted to do was crawl between the man's thighs, replace King's hand with his mouth. The look on King's face dared him to argue. He grabbed his cock and squeezed as he quickly made his way to his room.

12 King Was Going to Lose his Fucking Mind

King lay there waiting for Linc to come back with his cock hard and leaking onto his hairy belly. It seemed as if he'd waited forever until Linc padded back into the room. His cheeks were pink as he held a flesh colored dildo in his hands. He opened the drawer and pulled out the lube.

"Lie down with your head at the foot of the bed, put one leg over me so I can watch you get that inside your tight ass."

"King."

"Do as I say. Do you like some pain, baby."

"Yes."

"Show me," he ordered. He felt like a bastard, turned on by his man's embarrassment, but he didn't care. He wanted it all.

He held his breath as Linc positioned himself like he wanted Linc too. His fuzzy cheeks spread, he brought his hand to Linc's hole and teased the coarse curls. The muscles jumped under his fingertips. Linc's hands shook as the man spread lube onto his toy. Linc placed the blunt head and nudged, then Linc's hips were lifting and pushing himself onto the toy. A shuddered breath from Linc nearly had him coming when the head of the fake cock pushed inside.

He loved every inch of Linc, the curve of his belly, and the softness of his thighs. He wrapped his hand around the base of the cock that Linc was shallowly fucking into his ass. Linc's skin was already sweaty, and his cheeks flushed. He pushed and slammed the entire length into Linc's ass. The man's body bowed upward. He fucked his man hard and fast, listened to his pleas for mercy, but he didn't feel remorse or gentleness. He remembered the taste of Linc, the heat of Linc's abused cheeks, and the way the man humped the table wanting to get off.

That's what he wanted, Linc to lose his mind, no longer be held by steely control. He needed Linc to be mindless and in that moment, no other. There wasn't a time before this. No time they weren't together. His cock jerked and continued to leak as his man writhed on the bed. Meeting each brutal slam of the dildo. King only pushed and pulled harder as he took in the swollen and red rim that was taking a pounding. Linc begged for more, pleaded for harder.

"Tell me you want me to make it hurt."

"Make it hurt, please, fuck, King—"

Linc grabbed his legs behind his knees and pulled them to his chest. He'd never seen anything as beautiful.

"You want my cock, baby."

"Yes." Linc's answer was barely a hiss.

He roughly jerked the toy out, quickly sheathed his cock, and then Linc was on him. Desperate and shaking, and then his man was sliding down his dick. Strangling the fucking shaft. He cursed his broken leg because he wanted to push Linc to his back and fuck the man, make him scream and cry. Taste the tears on his cheeks. He wanted that—craved it.

"Ride me hard and fast. You can take it."

He pinched at Linc's hard nipples as the man bounced up and down. Linc's thighs were straining, and his hard, dripping dick was leaving wetness on both their bellies.

Stroking his hands down until he could wrap his hands around Linc's sides, his fingers digging into the softness. He loved it.

Linc's uninhibitedness was sexy as fuck. His head thrown back, his back arched, and the man rode him with abandon. Linc's skin was slick under his palms. He tightened his stomach muscles and curled upward to wrap his arms around Linc, and a strong embrace encircled his neck. Strong fingers sank into his damp hair, and he controlled Linc's movements. The man's ass was tight around his cock, and he pulled and pushed on and off his dick. His face was buried against Linc's throat, and Linc's chin rested on the top of his head.

"Fuck, that's s'good, baby, squeeze for me," he ordered, and Linc did as he asked.

They both grunted, and he didn't know how long he could last, so he forced a hand between their bodies and took Linc's cock in his hand. He jacked it in time with Linc taking his length. On every lift of Linc's body, the man tightened his ass nearly making him fucking come, but not until his man did. He'd waited too fucking long for this. He wanted everything his man could give him.

His free hand smoothed down Linc's back until his fingers bracketed his dick. The next downward movement, he pushed three fingers inside alongside his shaft.

"Like that, boy?" he asked.

"Uh huh." The words broke on a dirty little whimper until a scream broke the symphony of their grunts and moans while seed coated his hand and their bellies.

That's all it took, the sounds of his man getting off, the vice-like tightness around his fingers and dick, and he emptied into the condom. Then he collapsed back on the bed with Linc sprawled across his chest.

"I think you broke me," Linc's husky whisper fanned his sweaty chest.

He chuckled and eased from Linc's body. The man flinched, and he kissed Linc's shoulder, then the man's bearded cheek.

"In an hour, you'll be ready for round two."

"I'm going to go get something to clean us up. I'll be right back."

He felt a little smug as Linc struggled to get up and his legs seemed a bit wobbly. As Linc left the room, he closed his eyes and rubbed his hand through the come on his stomach. He was a sweaty mess, but he couldn't remember the last time he'd ever felt that relaxed.

His eyes popped open as Linc removed the condom and then gently cleaned him up. Even if his leg wasn't broken, he wouldn't have wanted to move. He studied Linc's face, the handsome features and the small crinkles at the corners of his eyes. He'd never seen a man he thought was more gorgeous than Linc was to him. He loved everything about him, the soft curve of his belly and the thick mat of hair that covered him from collarbones to waist. Loved the silver threading through it. The man took his fucking breath away from the minute he'd met him, and nothing had changed in the ten years that followed.

"Get in bed with me," he ordered he stretched his arm out and waited for Linc to take the spot beside him.

He held his breath until Linc was curled up to his side. That isn't something he'd done with anyone else. Linc was the only man he'd ever envisioned spending the night with and he wasn't going to let the opportunity pass by. He was secretly terrified that after the passion and lust faded, when the afterglow was gone, that Linc might panic and run from him.

No way could he handle that, so he tucked Linc tight against him and turned his head to brush a featherlight caress to Linc's forehead.

"Go to sleep, baby, I want to hold you while I sleep."

He smiled as he let his eyes drift closed and enjoyed the moment, inhaled the musk of Linc's scent. A perfect mix of man, sweat, and sex. Whatever happened in the morning, that right there, would be burned into his brain because it was his man. Tomorrow would take care of itself.

13 Morning After

Linc was terrified to move. King had him notched against his side, and he didn't want to ruin the moment. The night before was more than he'd ever dreamed of and he woke up to find that it was real. Part of him was having a bit of a meltdown yet the other eased into contentment. He finally had his man. A decade of unattainable fantasies of a life with King and it was all right there. His mouth pulled into a smile as he scrubbed his cheek on King's chest, and the thick hair teased his nose and lips. He tightened his arm around King, and he tensed as the man groaned.

"How long have you been awake?" King then brushed a kiss to his forehead.

"For a little while. I didn't move because I didn't want to wake you."

"Or were you having a little panic session?"

He wouldn't admit it for anything, but when he did wake up, he waited for that moment of fear. The one that said this was a one-night stand. He'd quickly swept the thought away. This was King. A man he'd secretly loved for nearly a decade.

"Asshole, I wasn't panicking. I was just enjoying the cuddling."

In his gut, he had a feeling King didn't exactly believe him. The thing about King was the man wouldn't call him on it. King always took into account his feelings. Always made sure he was okay even when King was out on the road.

"Well, honey, you can cuddle me anytime, anywhere."

"Are we good?"

"I thought last night was proof we were good."

"Think with a portion of your body that's not your dick, although, it probably takes up a majority of the blood supply." He snorted as King's chest puffed under his head.

"Aw, you're saying I have a big dick, ain't you a sweet talker."

"Of course you'd take that as a compliment."

"What man wouldn't take his man liking his dick as a compliment?"

"Okay, there is that."

"Totally going to throw out that toy now, nothing is better than the real thing, baby."

"I'll keep it for memories alone. I can't believe you made me do that."

"You know you fucking loved it."

He did. In his thirty-odd years, he'd never played with himself in front of anyone. Hell, he'd never gotten a spanking in his adult life. He rolled his eyes as he realized the list of what he hadn't done could get long if he thought about it too much.

"You're sleeping in my bed from now on." King's voice didn't offer room for argument.

"What about Mal? What are we going to tell him about Uncle Linc sleeping in his daddy's bed?"

He didn't know if he was ready to do the whole *I'm your daddy's boyfriend* conversation. Mal was a great kid. He understood that love was love, that King would one day get a boyfriend, and that Melanie would someday bring home a boyfriend or girlfriend. With the way the kid grew up and the extended family Mal had, he didn't really pay much attention to the husband or wife label.

"We'll tell him you're my partner just like Ben is Psycho's, or Scary and Tank are Elijah's. This doesn't have to be a big deal if we don't make it one. You know our kid doesn't worry about shit like that."

He rolled his lips between his teeth to hide his grin at King calling Mal their kid. It shouldn't be a surprise. Melanie and King had included him since Mal was born.

"I always thought about him as my kid. The moment I held him in the hospital is one of the best memories I've ever had."

"Are we done with all that doubting bullshit? Because I gotta tell you, you're stressing me out. I found a gray hair."

He turned his head and sat his chin on King's chest, he studied the dark strands and not one gray hair. He tugged the man's long goatee. "Well now that you mentioned it, there is that gray patch, right...there."

"What fucking gray patch?"

He started laughed as King tried to roll from the bed. He wrapped his arm around King and kept him lying down.

"You're so vain."

"How the hell am I supposed to be your boy toy with gray hair and all? You'll find a younger twenty-something model."

"Did we forget that you're only three months passed twenty-something?"

"True, I have at least another six months before I'm over the hill."

"I'm the one speeding toward forty."

"My sexy older man," King growled and pulled him onto his chest.

King's hands twisted in his hair and pulled his mouth down onto his roughly. It was out of control and hard, all tongue and teeth. His cock stiffened and pushed to King's naked hip. He combed his fingers through the thick mat of hair covering King's powerful chest and tugged, pinched King's pebbled nipple between his index and middle fingers.

He swallowed King's greedy sounds. He moaned as he slipped his hand beneath the sheet and fisted King's thick dick, squeezing as he jacked the length. King broke the kiss and pressed his head back into the mattress.

"Fuck, baby, don't stop," King pleaded.

King's big hand grabbed his ass cheek and forced him to rut against his hip. He sucked at the line of King's exposed throat. He was greedy. Years of denying who and what he wanted. King grunted and thrust shallowly in the tight clasp of his fingers.

"Goddamn, get your fucking ass up here." King scooted down the bed.

He didn't argue as he released King's length and shifted until he straddled King's face. His eyes rolled back in his head as King swallowed him whole. It took him a second to get his thoughts together. He wrapped his hand around the thick base and brought it to his lips.

He matched King lick for lick, suck for suck. He thrust repeatedly hitting the back of King's throat. Too soon his sac drew up, his skin tingled, and he ached so badly it was excruciating. He shook as his belly flattened to King's chest and his hips lifted and fell. He tongued the silky skin of King's cock, then pushed his tongue into the slit to taste the pre-come that flooded his mouth. He came with embarrassing quickness, and he hugged King's thighs as King came with a deep growl that teased his oversensitive dick.

Before he collapsed, he rolled to the side and onto his back to stare up at the ceiling. King's arm stretched out to hug the curve of his belly.

"That's the way to wake up. I require that every day."

He threw his forearm over his eyes and tried to catch his breath softly chuckling as King leisurely rubbed his hairy stomach. He barely moved as he felt King sit up.

"Hey, honey," King whispered.

"What?" He moved his arm just enough to peek at King out of one eye.

"Promise me you'll be in my bed every night and every morning."

Something about the look on King's face, the not so subtle insecurity, and he pushed up from the bed, resting his chin on King's shoulder.

"I wouldn't think of being anywhere else."

"I love you. I know I've told you for years, but I always meant it different than you took it."

He twined his right around King's neck and pressed their foreheads together. "I imagined you meant it differently. I love you too."

"Not exactly the way I imagined telling you. The leg fucked up my plan to take you out on dates and midnight rides. Slowly seduce you into loving me."

"You didn't have to seduce me. It was always there."

"I'm going to clean up and then make you breakfast."

"I'll make breakfast, and you handle the coffee. You're staying on that leg too much. I expect a ride soon. You haven't taken me since before Mal was born."

"I'll remedy that as soon as possible. Promise."

A tender kiss grazed his lips, and then King got up, used the crutches to head for the bathroom. He observed his man until King disappeared and he flopped back on the bed. The goofy grin he knew was on his face didn't faze him at all. King loved him. Wanted him and he wanted King. Finally, life was going the way it was supposed to. He sprawled out his limbs stretching wide before he rolled from bed and went to get breakfast started. They'd have to go get Mal soon.

14 So, I Can Call Him Daddy?

He finally wrenched his son away from Rage and Gunner. Fuck, it was like the twins were never going to see Mal again. He didn't give those little shits his back. He wouldn't put it past them to shiv him to get Mal back. He chuckled as he saw the mini-psychopaths plotting his demise from the front porch. Their arms crossed over their Brawlers t-shirts and their tiny fists clenched.

"I'd hurry up and strap Mal in," Linc whispered in his ear and smiled indulgently as the man watched Rage and Gunner.

Mal's big blue eyes hadn't left the porch. His son looked as heartbroken as the twins.

"Mal, you can play with them another day, I promise."

"I know, but I don't like when they're mad."

His kid was empathetic as hell. Mal picked up on moods quickly, and he was a natural nurturer. He actually balanced Rage and Gunner out.

"Do you ever think that we might have two sons-in-law when they get older?"

"Don't even think it. Can you imagine?"

He really couldn't, Rage and Gunner were a lot like Psycho, mini-replicas. Psycho had known Ben was his from the moment the giant spotted the cute baker. From that day forward Psycho was hopeless devoted. To be honest, he loved that his son had such close friends his own age. His son was a bit shy around kids other than the crew kids.

"I don't want to. My son isn't dating until he's fifty or I'm dead, so I don't have to deal with it."

"You're not going to be one of those dads, are you?"

"Yes, yes I am."

"Even if he turned out to like girls instead of boys?"

"Yes, even then."

Linc circled around the van, and he watched the man from the corner of his eye as Linc slipped into the front seat. He finished making sure Mal was secure. He closed the door and maneuvered himself into the passenger seat. His cast couldn't come off soon enough. He was getting tired of hobbling around and the non-stop itching. He also wanted to fuck his man when and where he wanted without having to think about his damn leg.

He fastened his seatbelt and leaned his head back on the rest.

"I saw you and Uncle Linc kissing."

Linc jerked but kept his gaze forward. He turned as far as he could in the seat. Mal was playing with a few toys cars running them up and down his extended legs.

"What do you think about that?"

Mal had a cute little scrunchy frown on his face. It was the look his son got when they were having serious conversations. Melanie, Linc, and he had always instilled a sense of safety where Mal could come to them for whatever. If anything bothered Mal, they wanted to know, and they needed Mal to understand nothing was off-limits. They'd decided to start early so that when the crazy teen years came around, he'd be comfortable in approaching them.

"I can call him Daddy?"

"Is that what you want?"

"He's like a Daddy. He tucks me in. Picks me up from daycare. Kisses my boo-boos. He takes care of me when you and Mom work."

"Why don't you ask him? I'm sure he'd love for you to call him Daddy."

"Uncle Linc?"

"Yes, Mal?"

"Can I call you Daddy Linc?"

King darted a glance to Linc as the man pulled to the side of the road. Tears were streaming down his cheeks to get caught in his closely trimmed beard. The man was out of the belt and squeezing through the small space between the seats. A huge smile curved his mouth even as tears slipped from the corners of his eyes as he watched Linc cup their son's face. Linc stared into the boy's eyes.

"I would love if you'd call me Daddy. You're one of the best things I've ever gotten in my life."

Linc hugged Mal to him, and Linc turned his head to look at him. The mouthed *thank you* was unnecessary. He was ecstatic that his family was officially whole.

"I can't breathe," Mal wheezed.

He chuckled as Linc released Mal and turned bright red.

"Sorry."

"That's okay, hugs mean you're happy right?"

He groaned since that was a Psycho question if he ever heard one. Maybe it was time to cut down on visits.

"Very happy. What do you say we go celebrate with ice cream?"

"Yes," Mal squealed.

He didn't take his eyes off Linc through the process of getting back in the driver's seat to the short trip to town to the ice cream shop. He didn't bother getting out, just opened the door and swung his legs out as Linc and Mal headed inside to order. He pulled his phone from his pocket and made the call he'd been waiting on.

"Is it time for Vegas?" Melanie's voice was almost as excited as Mal was for the ice cream trip.

"What if I said it was?"

"I'd say it was about fucking time, man. I'm so excited."

He could practically see Melanie doing her happy shimmy dance or what she called her fluffy girl excited dance. He wished he was as excited as she was. Years had passed with him imagining the day he'd get to ask Linc to marry him. A sliver of his heart taunted him with the fact his man could just say no. He didn't know if he could handle the rejection. To him, even all the times he'd denied his feelings and believing himself not good enough, they were meant to be. He couldn't picture his life with anyone else. While he'd rush the man to Vegas in a heartbeat, he wanted to do this right. If Linc wanted the wedding and all that, he'd do it. He loved that Linc wanted marriage and family.

"Do you think he'll say yes?"

"You bought the ring like stupid years ago. It's about time you pulled it out of hiding. And yes, I think he'll say yes."

"You have to come in this weekend. I want you here when I ask."

"I'll hit the bank to get the ring out of your safety deposit box. You never took the key back."

"Of course I didn't, all the important papers are in there in case something happened to me."

"The only thing that's going to happen to you is you're marrying the man of your dreams. I'll be there Saturday. I'll call Liv to give me a ride."

"Why Liv?" He hadn't known Liv and Melanie hung out.

"Don't even sound like that, that beast is as gay as they come. He's been on a job here and came in to have breakfast at the restaurant. I think he's headed home this weekend."

"See you Saturday then." Linc and Mal exited the front door, headed in his direction. "Shit, here comes Linc."

"Love you. You got this, man, Linc loves your hairy ass. Give our son a kiss for me. I can't wait to be done with school."

He didn't have time to say anything else before the call disconnected. Melanie hated being separated from Mal, but she was in nursing school, and not all of it could be done online. Less than a year and she'd be done with school, and she'd come home where she belonged. She'd even lined up a job with the local doctor.

"Melanie says she loves y'all."

"What's she up to?"

"The usual. She's coming home this weekend. Said Liv might give her a lift. He's in Atlanta for work."

"That will be great. It's been nice having her home more lately."

"Momma's coming home?"

He leaned down to scoop Mal into his arms and cuddled him to his chest. "She said I had to give you a kiss." He placed loud kisses all over Mal's face just like Melanie had done since he was born. Mal squealed and tried to get away. He finally took mercy on his kid and sat him down to enjoy his ice cream. "None for me?"

"You hate ice cream, which is unnatural."

"It's not unnatural. I just prefer a burger and fries over some cold ice cream cone."

"You don't know what you're missing."

He moaned as he watched Linc lick that damn treat and promised himself Linc was getting a spanking later for that impish twinkle in his gaze. He crossed his arms over his chest and watched the man in his life talk and laugh. For the first time, since he didn't know how long, he was content with his life. Knew exactly where he wanted to be and next time he had to leave for work, he knew that Linc would be waiting for him—hopefully with a ring on his finger.

15 What do You Say, Baby, Want to Make it Official?

Dinner was almost ready, and Melanie called to say she would be there any minute. He'd told her to invite Liv to stay to eat, but he had a feeling the man would say no. Liv was a nice guy if people looked past the scars, bastard attitude, and his tendency to punch first and ask questions later. Really that wasn't any different than any of the guys from the Crews. Although, as scary as they were, any of the guys he'd met since he became friends with them were the type to go out of their way to help their extended families.

A thrill worked down his spine at the strum of fingers over guitar strings. The sound was irresistible, and he rushed to the front porch. King was seated in one of the porch rockers, and his guitar hugged lovingly in his arms. He listened closely trying to pick out the tune, but Mal's attempt to copy King amused him. Mal had played the guitar since before he could walk. He'd so wanted to be like his daddy.

King went out the first time Mal showed interest and got Mal a guitar just like King's. Not some play one like he'd expected, but a real guitar—bigger than Mal. King's excitement that his son wanted to play was infectious. It was something Mal and King could share, and Mal's interested hadn't waned once.

He stepped off the porch, descended a few steps then sat down with his back to the porch support. *Tennessee Whiskey by Chris Stapleton*, that's what it was.

"Sing, I miss your voice," he implored.

"I sing and play for you every day."

"But you haven't done it today, please." King's deep baritone did it for him every time. He loved being center stage watching King do something he loved, but being able to sit on the front porch for a private show...that's what he lived for.

He held his breath as King adjusted his guitar and restarted the notes, then there it was. That voice that's made his heart kick into high gear so many times. He leaned his head back but didn't take his gaze from King and his man never stopped staring at him as he sang each word. He was about to melt into a very unmanly puddle, but, damn, that man, the whole package just did it for him.

Suddenly he had a lap full of little boy, and Mal leaned back against his chest as they listened to King play and sing. He glanced down to see Mal's eyes closed. He hugged Mal to his chest and went back to focusing on King.

Too soon the song ended, and when clapping erupted behind him, he turned to find Melanie and Liv.

"I don't see why the hell you still drive, man."

Liv sounded disgusted, but that wasn't unusual. The man sat across from him and leaned back. He was surprised Liv hadn't made a run for it yet.

"Because being gone a week at a time is better than being away from my family for months. They're more important, and besides, playing is fun, I ain't turning that shit into a job."

"And your man does enjoy how you give him private shows." Melanie smiled and kissed his cheek as she ascended the steps to hug King.

King set his guitar aside so that Melanie could curl up on his lap. He waited for a moment of jealousy but only laughed as his sister sighed.

"You'll have to play and sing some *Staind* for me before I go home. You haven't done it in forever."

"I promise, you'll get some Aaron Lewis. I know you just like to listen and imagine you're getting serenaded."

"You fucking know it. He's like the perfect man, but also if a cute little blonde comes along, I'd be happy too."

"What about the chick you went out with?" King casually asked.

Melanie hadn't dated much since the divorce, but there always seemed to be something off about the ones she did. Some weren't ready for the instant family. Others weren't too enthused about being best friends with the ex-husband. He worried about Melanie being lonely. She worked and went to school, then came home every weekend she could. His sister deserved to find someone of her own.

"No-go, chemistry was there when we met, but during dinner, I could see her as a friend to hang out with. Let me get through school, and I'll see about finding my person."

"You got plenty of time, and you'll be home soon."

"Yeah, plenty of time."

The longing in Melanie's voice broke his heart, but she hid it quickly with a smile and came over and plucked Mal from his lap.

"Linc, come here." King held out his hand.

The sad expression on Melanie's face changed to a bright happiness so quickly the shift made him dizzy.

"Go," Melanie ordered and grabbed his hand forcing him to stand.

"You're being weird," he whispered as he approached King and took the man's calloused hand. The roughness caused a shiver to move up and down his spine.

"Now, I was hoping I could do this a little different, but me getting down on one knee isn't possible, so this'll have to work."

A box opened and he forgot to breathe. Two matching bands were nestled inside, simple silver wedding rings.

"Don't say this is quick, we've known each other for almost a decade. I've waited so long to be able to announce to everyone you're mine, but when I do that, I want my ring on this finger." King punctuated the statement by brushing a kiss to his ring finger.

"King—"

"No, please, let me finish. You've been everything to me even when the guilt ate at me, but the day I met you this was the only way it could end. You here, in our home, with our son, and I don't want to wait. There's not a lot I'm sure of in life, but you being mine is as solid as it gets. So, what do you say, baby, want to make it official? Please, marry me."

He pinched his thigh with his free hand, and it hurt so he couldn't be dreaming. King looked like he was about to lose his mind. He dropped to his knees next to the chair and grabbed King's scruffy cheeks, then pulled the man's face to his. He kissed him, tasted salty tears and didn't know if they were King's, his, or a combination of both.

Their movements were unhurried, sweet and tender. He whispered against King's mouth, "Yes."

"About fucking time."

He glanced at Liv and found the man scrubbing his hands over his face. Relief etched into his scarred features like it was Liv waiting for the answer. His attention was drawn away from Liv as cool metal slid onto his finger for the first time and he knew the last. King was it. There wasn't another man for him. He didn't care if it was quick or if they'd dated for years, the only thing that mattered was it was right.

"I love you."

"I love you too. So, the question is how fast can you pack for Vegas?"

"Vegas? What if I want the long engagement and ceremony, all that stuff?"

King groaned and tipped his head all the way back. He held in his laughter at the pained expression.

"If that's what you want, then that's what you get."

"Fuck that, let's go to Vegas."

King's mouth slammed onto his, and it wasn't like the kiss of moments ago. The kiss was a claiming and he was completely okay with that.

16 Vegas, Here We Come!

Bags littered their bed. Linc had already packed Mal's, and all that was left was a bag for them, then they were off to Vegas. Sin and Saint had already filed a flight plan and were waiting out at the private airstrip their stepfather Ernie had outside town near Pelter's place. It was a six-seater, so, not everyone could come, but everyone had told him the party would be out of control when they came back. Peaches and Lily, the matriarchs of the Crews, weren't exactly happy with the Vegas deal.

Lily had performed every ceremony since the first crew member Berzerker married his man years ago. He felt bad for robbing her of the moment, but Lily liked a production, and he and Linc just wanted something simple. Them, Melanie, and Mal, along with Liv and the twins, and the twins were flying them out. Also, the twins were looking forward to a few days in Vegas. Well, Sin was, Saint just wanted an excuse to fly.

"You sure about this, King?"

"Why do you keep asking that?"

"Because, I don't know, I'm sort of freaking out."

He flinched. Was he pushing Linc into marrying him too quickly? Maybe his man wanted all those things that went along with getting hitched? The ceremony and the reception, the honeymoon after all the planning.

"No, not like that." Linc crawled across the bed and straddled his lap.

He gripped Linc's hips and looked up at his man, his husband-to-be. So much had changed in a short period of time, could Linc feel pressured?

"I want to marry you, sooner the better, but I feel bad. Lily and Peaches live for these moments of marrying their boys off, and here we are robbing them of it. I know it's stupid to feel guilty, but I do."

"We promised them they could throw the biggest reception in the history of Powers when we come back in a few days. Lily and Peaches just want us to be happy. I feel guilty a bit too. So, let's get finished packing so we can get to Vegas and get back to make the matriarchs happy."

He knew he didn't soothe away all of Linc's guilt, but maybe he'd assuaged a bit of it. They were already dressed in their suits. Linc looked handsome, and he couldn't believe his man said yes—that Linc would be his forever. He looked down at himself and groaned, the pant leg was split to allow for his cast and pinned at the ankle, but he was not going to get married in exercise shorts.

"Remember when you and Melanie got married," Linc asked getting off his lap.

"She was wearing a hot pink tank top and cut-off jeans, with flip flops, and I had on jeans and a Metallica t-shirt. Twenty minutes at the county courthouse and we were back to work. Your parents refused to show up. Did you want—"

He knew what was going to come out of Linc's mouth as soon as Linc interrupted him. Linc's parents were traditional, and they hated the way Melanie, him, and Linc were raising Mal. If it wasn't for Peaches and her threats that she'd ruin Linc's parents, they would've probably tried to take Mal from them a long time ago.

"King, do you think my parents would come to watch me get married to a man? They're going to be scandalized when they learn I'm sleeping with my ex-brother-in-law."

"I'm going to be your husband, and they don't need to be here."

"What about Bear? Wouldn't you like him to be your best man?"

"I already talked to Bear, and he said he'd give us a honeymoon for a present, just do whatever made us happy. He couldn't be happier for us."

"Has he wrangled Mary yet?"

That was a long, sad story, and he felt sorry for Bear. The man was in love with the woman. "He thought he had, but she'd refused to see him the last month or so. He's fucking miserable. I've never heard him that down. You know how Bear is."

"The always bubbly gentle giant. He has no idea why she won't see him?"

"None. They'd made this list of things Mary missed out on and always wanted to do. They were working through the list and all of a sudden, she stopped answering his calls. Joker won't even let Bear near the garage office so Bear can apologize for whatever he did."

"They'll work it out. Maybe it was too much for Mary. She hasn't had a lot of good in her life. It could've been too much too soon."

"Hope so, but enough about my uncle's tragic love life. We ready?"

"As ready as I think we'll ever get." Linc zipped the bag closed and slipped the strap over his shoulder. Mal and Melanie were waiting in the living room. It had been two days since Linc said yes because it had taken a little bit for Sin and Saint to make arrangements. They would've been happy getting a regular flight, but the twins had insisted, and he'd noticed Linc wasn't good at telling the cute little Twinks no especially when they started batting their pretty blues at him. Linc was a total pushover.

He used his crutches to get up and again, couldn't wait to get rid of them and the damned cast. He hated being away from Linc and Mal, but he had to get back to work. With picking up a gig here and there for the extra money and his benefits, they weren't hurting. It wasn't the same amount coming in though, and he still had a family to provide for. Melanie shouldn't have to work her ass off like he did.

He cleared his head of everything but the fact he was getting ready to marry his man. He entered the living room behind Linc. Mal bounced in his tiny suit they'd gotten him. Hell, even Liv cleaned up well. That was one expensive suit that had dollar signs floating around the designer threads.

"We ready to do this damn thing, gentleman? It's about time you made an honest man out of my brother." Melanie bounced around with Mal on her hip.

She looked beautiful in a peach-colored sundress. Her hair up and flowers woven into the dark honey curls. It was a Lily special, the same style Lily wore when she performed the ceremonies.

"You look stunning, Melanie." He approached her, set his crutches aside and gave her a tight squeeze. Mal trapped between them protesting being smashed.

"Thanks, you're not too bad yourself."

Melanie hated compliments on her looks. She's always been a little on the curvy side, but since Mal, she'd filled out and was a little self-conscious about the extra weight. His best friend was always on a diet, and she didn't need to be.

"Ready to be my best lady?"

"I've been ready for years," she whispered as she gave him one more hug.

"Your ride awaits. The twins texted to say they were gassed up and ready to go whenever we got there," Liv announced and headed for the door.

They all quickly followed, wanting to get in the air as soon as possible. He was impatient to say I do to his man and have Linc have his name. They'd discussed it, and as much as he wanted Linc to have his name, he wanted the man to be happy, and luckily Linc loved the sound of Lincoln King. Linc said he was his family and he wanted to have his name, the same as Melanie and Mal had.

They piled into Liv's massive SUV and pulled out toward their destination. In a matter of hours, every dream he'd ever had would come true, and he couldn't fucking wait.

17 Kidnapped!

Flying always made Linc sick, and he was there with his head between his knees, trying to keep the little he'd put in his stomach that day stay down. King was rubbing his back from his seat across the narrow aisle, but he had a feeling the little plane was worse than a jet. Claustrophobia and air sickness, just what he fucking needed before getting goddamned married.

Mal was having the time of his life. Sin had actually given up his co-pilot seat and headset to Mal. Although he wanted Mal to have fun, he threatened Saint's life if he even thought about giving the controls to a four-year-old. He didn't give a shit if Saint had learned to fly at Mal's age or not.

"Are we there yet?"

"Baby, we've only been in the air twenty minutes. Why don't you lean your head back, close your eyes and see if you can get some sleep?"

They were about to have their first fight. That voice, while he assumed it was supposed to be soothing, was actually annoying as hell.

"I don't need sleep. I need this damn plane to land."

"Saint wants to do some tricks," Sin said sweetly, but the little shit was demented.

How the hell had he ever thought the twins were cute?

"He better not fucking dare!"

Sin just laughed, but Linc glared daring anyone else to even think about it. He grabbed King's cast covered knee as they seemed to lose altitude quickly.

"What the hell is that?" he demanded and jerked his head up, regretting it instantly.

He knew Saint was one of the best, learning to fly since he was three, seated on his stepfather's lap, but that didn't mean accidents didn't happen, and there he was in small ass plane headed hundreds of miles to get married.

"I'm going to die before we get married," he muttered miserably.

"No, you're not. If I didn't trust Saint, our family wouldn't be on this plane. I promise, we'll be fine."

"Okay, lady and gentleman, we have a bit of a problem," Saint hollered from his seat in the cockpit.

"I told you," he whined.

"We're going to need to land."

"Go get Mal," King told Sin.

"No, the landing is easy, but don't be mad at us, okay, they threatened to do terrible things to us."

He studied the young man and saw guilt etched into the feminine features. He almost felt bad for thinking terrible things about the boy.

"Who?" he asked.

"Peaches and Lily." Everyone on the plane except King answered.

"Lily couldn't allow you to get married in Vegas by strangers. This is a family thing, and we all wanted to be there for it. See you two walking down the aisle and hear the I dos."

The plane smoothly descended onto a smooth patch of land, and he couldn't tell where they were.

"Camden's place. We made a few circles to kill time, and he offered his yard. We've worked our asses off for two days since Liv gave us the heads up."

"Y'all were in on this?" He carefully turned around to find Liv and Melanie shrugging.

"Bear wanted the honor of giving you away to welcome you to the family. This should be a family thing, and we all knew y'all didn't want to plan a whole big production. It's nothing fancy. It'll be as quick as if you were going to Vegas. Camden has all the paperwork. We had a clerk loosen the rules for us about the license and all that."

Melanie had spoken so quickly most of her words ran together. He couldn't believe what they'd done. As they landed, he looked out the window to see twinkle lights everywhere. Candles burned along the walkway between a grouping of chairs. Tables were set up and even an area where he assumed the Executioners would be playing at some point.

The plane rolled to a stop, and Sin jumped up to open the door. Scary and Tank jogged forward to help King out of the plane. Lily and Peaches were dressed in flowing hippie style dresses, flowers in their hair, and sweet motherly smiles on their mouths.

He was thankful when his feet hit solid ground, and he turned to help Melanie down, then took Mal from Saint. Liv held onto Saint until the boy's feet hit the ground. Liv barely got his shoulders free of the plane—the big man had to turn sideways.

King was beside him with a strong arm around his waist as he let his eyes move around the yard. Everyone was there, the Twirled, Brawlers, Executioners, and even the Trenton Security Crew, partners, and kids ran around the yard. He placed Mal on his feet, and the boy was instantly on the move to find the rest of the kids.

"What did y'all do?"

He turned to find King watching him with a loving expression, and it was almost too much. What these people, his chosen family had done for him—them—he didn't know what to say. It was perfect.

"Well, Lily ambushed me in my office." Pelter stepped forward. "Said we had an emergency, two of her boys were getting married without her, and that couldn't happen. So, let's just say, we begged, bribed and mostly threatened to get everything ready before Eric and Ellison were due to fly y'all out."

"You didn't have to go—"

"You stop right fucking there," Peaches and Lily stepped forward as they spoke in unison.

"There ain't much we can't do, and we could've let y'all take off to Vegas for a big flashy wedding, but Peaches and me, you're our boys and getting married is a family affair. We were all trying to get to Vegas, but we wouldn't all get there in time, but marrying people is my thing, Linc, *mine*, that shit you don't take from me."

"We did feel guilty."

"Fucking right y'all did. I haven't *not* married any of the boys. We've planned every one to make it perfect, and we weren't missing out on this or the party after. I even went out and got special party favors. So, you two are getting hitched, then we're going to smoke and drink until we pass out where we fall. Except for Twitch, Elijah, and Gregory who are taking all the kids for the evening."

"They ain't taking them far. My fucking house looks like a daycare center." Pelter almost sounded offended, but there was a smile on his face. "Rage and Gunner have already expressed their displeasure at the fact I have red meat in my fridge. They were about to throw out every animal by-product in my house."

The happiness the Sheriff was displaying was weird and slightly disturbing. Where was the Pelter scowl? He glanced passed the big man to see Sin and Saint staring at the man like he was the Goddess' gift to man. Those two were in for a heartache. Pelter had been keeping them at a distance, and he didn't see that changing anytime soon.

"Well, you wanted it quick, so let's do this. Bear is waiting on the porch for you, Linc, so he can walk you down the aisle. King, Melanie is going to help you to the altar. Let's get you hitched so you can get your first fuck in as husband and husband." Lily clapped her hands together.

King's fingertips stroked his cheek, and he turned to him.

"Is this okay? We can still make a run for Vegas."

"No, this is perfect, this is what I wanted. I would've married you in Vegas, but I couldn't imagine not being surrounded by family. Thank you for this, without you, I wouldn't have Mal, you, and—" He turned to scan the yard. "All of them."

"Then I'll see you in a few minutes." King started to lean in, and a loud whistle distracted them.

"Save that shit for after the I dos, or I'll make your fucking life hell," Lily ordered as her husband came up and offered his arm, then led her toward the lighted platform where he'd marry King.

Melanie stepped up to King's side, and they followed after Lily and Damon. Everyone else cleared out, and he strode toward where Bear waited for him. The big man met him halfway.

"Don't you look handsome all dressed up?"

"Thanks," Bear said, but the normally happy man seemed troubled.

"Want to talk about it?"

"No, Mary made her decision, and I promised her that I'd take whatever she allowed me. I was just hoping for more time. But tonight isn't about me. It's about you and King. I wanted to welcome you to the King family and the extended craziness that comes with it. I'm so proud of King, the family he created with you, Mal, and Melanie. He's loved you for so long, Lincoln Church, and that man is lucky beyond the stars that you love him back. Here." Bear handed him a box.

He took it and opened it to find a beautiful braided ring inside.

"It's gorgeous."

"It was my father's. He passed it on to me one night over drinks a few days before he died. He told me I'd know what to do with it when the time came. I had it resized for King. Dad would've been sitting in the first row to watch his only grandchild get married, beaming with pride and I'm so fucking proud. This ring was on my dad's finger for over sixty years, and he loved my mom just as much the day he died as he did the first time he laid eyes on her in white. I give it to you hoping some of that happiness makes it to another generation."

He held the box so tight his hand hurt, and he felt his eyes sting. But Bear didn't say anything, just turned and held out his arm.

"May I have the honor of giving you away to the luckiest man on the planet right now?"

"Bear, thank you."

"No need for thanks, you just love hard and long and never take that for granted."

"I promise."

He took a deep breath as he walked arm in arm with Bear toward his future. Mal stood in front of King, and Melanie wiped tears from her eyes as she rested her cheek against King's bicep. Everyone stood as he made his way down the walkway, and he couldn't wait to say I do.

Bear handed him over to King, and he looked into the man's beautiful eyes, took in the adoration aimed at him, and didn't realize until that moment how lucky he was.

18 Lullabies and Encores

Linc's head rested on his chest, and King combed his fingers through the softness of his damp blond hair. His man kept brushing kisses to his chest. He inhaled the scent of soap and shampoo. They'd cleaned up and got in bed, no words were exchanged, but he felt Linc's smile. They'd made love for hours and were now settled into Tank's cabin. The silent man offered the place for a weekend honeymoon until they could take the trip Bear had given them.

"What are you thinking about?" He wanted to know what was making Linc happy so he could do it again.

"You."

"Care to elaborate?"

He laced his fingers through Linc's and kissed the new ring. He placed the man's hand on his chest and covered it with his. Last year when he tried to imagine what this year would bring, this isn't where he saw himself. The only sure thing he'd been sure of was that another year would pass and Linc wouldn't be his—he'd have to watch the man and forever be forced to keep his distance.

"How I got lucky enough to get you to propose."

"I bought the ring right after the divorce."

"What?" Linc turned to prop his chin on his chest.

"After the divorce became final. I was on a stop, and I just had lunch when I passed by this jewelry store. In the window, there were these two men's wedding bands, and I saw you wearing it. I went inside and bought them, still knowing that I'd never have you. I tucked them away in my safety deposit box. Melanie and I got so drunk one night, Mal was with Bear and you were still dating that guy you were seeing. I confessed I'd bought the rings and who I bought them for."

"Did she think we—"

"No, we weren't happy as a couple, but cheating wasn't in either of us. We loved each other, just not like we were supposed to. That night she gave me permission."

"Permission?" Linc asked as he rubbed his fingers through his chest hair.

"Yeah, to be happy, but you were with what's his name and had been for a few years. I loved you enough for you to be happy so I just got used to pretending. Then I became the flirt and the easy fuck, but I wasn't. I'm not saying I was a monk, but I sure as hell wasn't as bad as some thought."

"I couldn't expect you to stay celibate, I sure as hell hadn't, and I wasn't exactly over the whole my sister slept with the man I was in love with thing."

He chuckled and shook his head. "That was a bit of a hurdle."

"I hate all the years we lost, but I don't think I would've done anything differently. Neither of us were ready, and this right here is perfect."

"Did you want more kids?"

"Do you?"

"I don't know. Mal's about to go to school, and I'm still sticking with the driving. Melanie pulled me aside tonight and offered to act as a surrogate if we wanted her to."

"Why don't we get used to the family right now? Melanie's coming home next Summer for good, and she might meet someone. Today I can say I'm happy with the four of us."

"I agree, but I wanted you to know the option was there."

"And I love you for it, but do you know what I want more than anything?"

"Oh, and what's that?"

"Lullabies, I had to share my usual nightly solo show with others. As my wedding gift from you, I want a song." Linc surged from the bed and ran out of the room.

Linc returned a few minutes later with his guitar and pick, and held it out in front of him. He scooted up until he was leaned back against the headboard. Linc adjusted the pillow under his cast. He knew the perfect song because it was one of Linc's favorites. Placing the calloused pads on the strings, he eased it to the melody. He almost missed starting the song as Linc sighed.

He began to sing *Etta James' At Last,* and as always, he kept his gaze on Linc. Didn't matter if they were in the same room and all alone or in a crowded bar, he sang for Linc because it made his man happy. He regretted not being able to dance his man around the room as he sang the words low into his man's ear, but soon he'd remedy that.

As the last word left his mouth and he stopped playing, Linc got onto his knees. His man removed the instrument and set it gently on the bed beside them.

"Now, I want another song, but this time you're gonna sing it to me while you're inside me."

Linc straddled his lap, and they groaned as Linc held his cock and slid down the length. He was tight and hot, perfect, and made just for him.

"What do you want me to sing, baby?" he asked as he stroked his hands from Linc's lower back to curve around the man's shoulders.

He flexed and slammed Linc down until he was ball's deep. They arched into each other, and any thought of singing left his head.

"Loving you," Linc whispered with a sigh.

"You want Paolo Nutini?" He'd sing fucking opera if it made his man happy.

"Yes, sing it," his man demanded.

"If you have a thing for pretty, skinny dudes, what the fuck you doing with me?"

"Shut up and sing for me. I'm going to turn into a very demanding husband."

"As you wish." And he sang as his man rode him slowly.

Some of the words came out as groans and others he forgot to sing at all, but what his man wanted, his man got. He sang softly into Linc's ear as they lazily came together. No hurrying to the finish because they had all the time in the world to be together. He fisted his fingers in Linc's hair and roughly tugged the man's head back as he paused to suck at the strong column of Linc's neck. He didn't give a fuck that the song took three times as long, all he cared about was the sexy little whimpers and the pleas for him to love his man.

The slow pace took its toll, and he broke as he slipped his arm around Linc's ass, then flexed to increase his man's pace until neither of them could breathe. Linc's lips came down on his, brushing as they moved. They gasped and grunted, clutched at each other as Linc's cock, trapped between their bodies, jerked and heat spread between them. He let out a long moan as he took Linc's hips in a bruising grip and forced the man to ride him faster and harder until he came with a shout muffled against his man's mouth.

"Want another song?" he asked as he smiled against Linc's lips.

"Give me a few minutes. I think my ass might need a break."

"Well, Mr. King, whenever you're ready for an encore you just let me know."

The sound of Linc's laughter made him happier, and he'd spend the next fifty plus years making sure his man had all the smiles and songs he needed.

"I do love your encores, but let me get you cleaned up."

He reluctantly let Linc go and couldn't take his gaze away from his man. Ten years he'd waited for this and never once would he let his man regret saying yes.

Epilogue: Perfection in All the Broken Pieces

Thanksgiving

"Put the turkey down, you heathens," Lily yelled as she chased Rage and Gunner as they took off with the roasting pan held between them.

Linc jumped out of the way before the twin terrors could take him out at the knees. He spun the ring on his finger as he went in search of his new husband. Three weeks had passed since they'd said I do in Pelter's front yard, and they were back because Pelter's house was the only one big enough for all of them to get together for Thanksgiving.

The Crews were big on holidays, but they made sure they took the opportunity to get together every chance they got and holidays were a good time for that. All the couples and triads were cuddled up together as they waited for the turkey to be hunted down although no one was in much of a hurry.

As always, Peaches was perched on Gib's lap, and he had his hand under her flowing linen skirt. He smiled as he shook his head. Gib's touch wasn't altogether innocent, and he knew they'd disappear before dinner, then wouldn't show up again until Gib made sure Peaches was flushed and smiling.

Pelter was in the kitchen trying to keep Sin and Saint in line, but he told that man it was a full-time job. Pelter denied it was his responsibility. There was one thing the man couldn't deny though; his gaze never left Sin and Saint. Sooner or later, Pelter was going to give in, and he hoped the pretty, blond twins could handle it. He headed for the front door because he knew that was where he'd find the Executioners.

He pushed open the door and found King, Joker, and Ghost playing and singing. Dem was tucked between Joker's legs, his head rested on the man's thigh, and he couldn't be happier for Joker. The man deserved love.

Ghost was playing his keyboard with Harper, his pretty little wife, draped over his back. The newest addition to the Executioners Crew in a travel bassinet. Erika had arrived a few weeks early but was ginger perfection. Lou, Lucky's sister, said that as it was, the Crews could breed without her help. Her womb space was no longer available.

He smiled as he stepped forward and took the rocker beside King. The man didn't even pause playing as King leaned sideways and stole a kiss.

He glanced at the door as Sin and Saint appeared, then they took a seat and joined in on the harmony. The twins held hands drawing comfort from each other. They liked to joke about being friends from the womb.

He took the time to study the men and woman that he was connected to. Each one had their own demons they dealt with, but they all relied on each other.

This was his family, his happily ever after, and he loved the perfection in all the broken pieces, and they were beautiful.

THE END

About the Author

By day, J.M. is an introverted cook hiding out in her kitchen in the middle of nowhere Ohio, by night and any free time she may have, she is a writer of mainly LGBTQ Fiction and Erotica. Although. she's equal opportunity when it comes to telling a story, she'll even write a bit of straight erotic romance when the mood strikes.

She has been writing for years in old notebooks. At the age of eight, she wrote the worst poem in the history of poetry, but it sparked her love for writing. She reads too much and loves to get lost in other worlds and her favorite stories have to include laughter and having the reader doing at least one double take. Thirty-something, forever restless she uses her stories to ground herself, and find her place of peace.

WHERE TO FIND J.M.
www.jmdabneyauthor.com

www.ingramcontent.com/pod-product-compliance
Lightning Source LLC
Chambersburg PA
CBHW060936120626
46557CB00003B/1015